PUFFIN CANADA

JUST DESERTS

ERIC WALTERS is the highly acclaimed and best-selling author of over sixty novels for children and young adults. His novels have won the Silver Birch Award, the Red Maple Award, as well as numerous other prizes, including the White Pine, Snow Willow, Tiny Torgi, Ruth Schwartz and IODE Violet Downey Book Awards, and have received honours from the Canadian Library Association Book Awards, The Children's Book Centre and UNESCO's international award for Literature in Service of Tolerance.

Also by Eric Walters from Penguin Canada

The Bully Boys
The Hydrofoil Mystery
Trapped in Ice
Camp X
Royal Ransom
Run
Camp 30
Elixir
Shattered
Camp X: Fool's Gold
Sketches
The Pole
The Falls
Voyageur
Black and White
Wounded
Camp X: Shell Shocked
Camp X: Trouble in Paradise
Fly Boy

sandstorm, the oasis, a magical evening under the stars with our guides playing music and singing songs, and a tremendous thunderstorm.

As our party ran each day I walked. Often I would start first, pointed in a general direction, and then I would be overtaken by the runners within a few kilometres. On some days I caught them by lunch, as they slept to avoid the high-noon sun, and I'd keep going. On one day I found myself far ahead, out of contact with anybody for hours, and realized that I was "lost" in the desert. I started to walk back into my tracks before I found they had been blown away. I stood there, figuring out how much water I still had, how long I could survive on my own, and then waited. As I waited I pulled out my little writing pad and made the notes that became the basis for my character in the book becoming lost.

This novel is finished but Ray's adventures are ongoing. His new book, *Running to Extremes: Ray Zahab's Amazing Ultramarathon Journey* (written with Steve Pitt; Penguin, 2011), is the ultimate, most up-to-date account of Ray's epic journeys. He continues his quest not only to push the envelope of what is possible but also to educate and inspire students around the world. He invites schools to get involved through Impossible2Possible, to come along for these trips, and to share the message, the realization, that almost nothing is impossible.

Just Deserts

ERIC WALTERS
with Ray Zahab

PUFFIN
CANADA

PUFFIN CANADA

Published by the Penguin Group

Penguin Group (Canada), 90 Eglinton Avenue East, Suite 700,
Toronto, Ontario, Canada M4P 2Y3 (a division of Pearson Canada Inc.)

Penguin Group (USA) Inc., 375 Hudson Street, New York, New York 10014, U.S.A.
Penguin Books Ltd, 80 Strand, London WC2R 0RL, England
Penguin Ireland, 25 St Stephen's Green, Dublin 2, Ireland
(a division of Penguin Books Ltd)
Penguin Group (Australia), 250 Camberwell Road, Camberwell, Victoria 3124,
Australia (a division of Pearson Australia Group Pty Ltd)
Penguin Books India Pvt Ltd, 11 Community Centre, Panchsheel Park,
New Delhi – 110 017, India
Penguin Group (NZ), 67 Apollo Drive, Rosedale, Auckland 0632, New Zealand
(a division of Pearson New Zealand Ltd)
Penguin Books (South Africa) (Pty) Ltd, 24 Sturdee Avenue, Rosebank,
Johannesburg 2196, South Africa

Penguin Books Ltd, Registered Offices: 80 Strand, London WC2R 0RL, England

First published 2011

1 2 3 4 5 6 7 8 9 10 (WEB)

Manufactured in Canada.

LIBRARY AND ARCHIVES CANADA CATALOGUING IN PUBLICATION

Walters, Eric, 1957-
Just deserts / Eric Walters and Ray Zahab.

ISBN 978-0-14-317935-1

I. Title.

PS8595.A598J98 2011 jC813'.54 C2011-902082-3

Visit the Penguin Group (Canada) website at **www.penguin.ca**

Special and corporate bulk purchase rates available; please see
www.penguin.ca/corporatesales or call 1-800-810-3104, ext. 2477 or 2474

For my wife Kathy and for my friend and fellow runner
Patrick Doyle

CHAPTER ONE

WHAT WAS THAT SOUND, and why was it *so* loud? It felt like somebody was pounding on the inside of my head with a sledgehammer or—no ... it was the door. Okay, now I had *three* questions: *who* was pounding on the door, *why* were they pounding so hard, and finally, was the person who was doing the pounding small enough that I could inflict serious injury on him?

The pounding kept coming, and it was getting even louder. Each crash against the door sent a corresponding pain shooting into my head, like a knife being plunged into my brain.

"Ethan, open up!"

The voice was familiar, although at that moment I couldn't quite place its owner. All I knew was that I truly wanted to kill him ... assuming I could do it really quietly.

Instead I rolled over and pulled the pillow over my head, but the pounding came again, and the pillow was about as helpful as a Band-Aid on a shotgun wound. That's what it felt like, as if somebody had shot me in the head. I would have almost welcomed that. One shot to the head to end the pain.

I really had to stop drinking. Or at least stop drinking so much—that was more realistic. I'd remind myself not to drink so much. Then again, if drinking killed brain cells, obviously I wouldn't remember the reminder, so—

"Ethan, wake up!" the voice bellowed.

Why wasn't he giving up? Wait, it was a different voice now. Either there were two of them, or they were pounding in relays.

There was only one way to make it stop. I'd have to kill him ... them. On the bright side, it would be justifiable homicide. Pounding on the door of a guy who was suffering a blinding, head-splitting hangover was definitely asking for it. Or I could plead temporary insanity—the insanity of the person trying to wake me up!

He pounded again, and I rolled over and tried to jump out of bed. The sudden change of elevation sent my head reeling and my stomach lurching. I put a hand down on the night table to steady myself and looked at the clock. It was just before eight-thirty—eight-thirty in the morning! What sort of heartless, brainless idiot would pound on my door at this time on a Sunday morning?

I staggered forward and— "Ugggh!"

I looked down and lifted up my foot. Vomit dripped off my toes into a puddle on the floor. I could only hope that it was at least *my* vomit. Somehow that would make it a little less disgusting.

I dropped my foot to the carpet and dragged it along, trying to wipe off the vestiges of puke that clung to it. It wasn't like it was going to do much damage to this carpet. It was worn, ugly and tasteless—like everything else at this school.

There was the sound of a key clicking against the lock—whoever it was, he was trying to get into my room. Saved me the trouble of staggering over to open the door.

Donovan, followed by Clive, poked his head into my room. I knew them, but that didn't mean I liked them or would spare them from death or—

"Are you all right?" Donovan asked.

"One of us is going to be fine," I snapped. "Do you know what time it is?"

"It's just before nine in the morning," Clive answered.

"And don't you think that might be a little early to be banging on somebody's dormitory door on a Sunday morning?"

"Sunday?" Donovan sounded confused.

"It's *Monday* morning," Clive said.

"Yeah, right, it's Monday ... quit screwing around."

"No, seriously, it's Monday."

"It is," Donovan added. "Honestly."

"This isn't April first, and I'm no fool," I snapped. Bad enough waking me up without trying to make me look like an idiot. "Go away and leave me alone, and don't come back until it really *is* Monday."

"No, it *is* Monday," Donovan insisted.

He stepped back and pushed the door wide open. Beyond him, I could see that the hallway was filled with students in uniform, carrying books, on their way to classes.

I was shocked.

"But what happened to Sunday?" I gasped.

"Sunday happened. You missed it. You must have slept through it or something."

Sleep, no. *Something,* yes. I remembered Saturday night, being out at a party and ... I didn't really remember getting home, but obviously I had. But zoning out all of Sunday? I'd passed out before, even forgot part of an evening, but to lose an entire day ... that was different.

Either way, it didn't really matter. Class was going to be starting in less than thirty minutes, and I'd already been warned that the next time I was late I'd be facing major disciplinary action.

So the guys hadn't been harassing me so much as helping me. I could have thanked them, maybe, but ... whatever. It wasn't like they were my friends.

"I'd better get dressed fast and get to class before—"

"No, you're not supposed to go to class," Donovan said.

Now I was even more confused.

"Headmaster McWilliams wants to see you," Clive explained.

"In his office," Donovan added.

"Why does he want to see me?"

"He didn't exactly tell us, but he didn't look particularly happy."

"Does he *ever* look happy?" I asked.

"Never," Donovan agreed. "But I've been around here for five years, and I've learned that keeping him waiting is not going to make him any happier."

"Well, I guess he'll learn that you don't always get what you want," I said, trying to sound casual. "Tell him I'll be there when I'm ready."

They both looked shocked.

"You want us to tell him *that*?" Clive asked.

"Don't worry about it. He'll figure it out when I'm not there immediately. Just go to class and I'll take care of it."

I could tell by their expressions that they were surprised *and* impressed.

"I need to get dressed, and I'm not planning on putting on a show, so you two have to leave," I said as I shooed them out, closing the door behind them.

I slumped against the door. Damn, this was serious. But how serious, and what was the headmaster upset about? It wasn't that I hadn't done anything wrong. The question was, what had he found out about? Drinking alcohol, on or off school premises, was a big deal if you got caught. It was very definitely against the rules, so that could be a problem ... and I guess whatever happened on the day I couldn't remember. But really, other than vomiting, I'd probably just slept Sunday away.

In any event, what I needed to do was to get to his office as quickly as possible, looking as together as possible. Unfortunately the two things worked against each other. I had a choice: be fast or be presentable. I'd at least have to be in uniform, have my tie on straight—he was a fanatic about fixing people's ties. I thought it had to do with the fact that he liked to wrap his hands around people's necks, like he was choking the life out of them—that was something he really enjoyed doing.

I'd wash my face, throw on my uniform, fix my tie, but first ... I ran off to the washroom, practically tumbling over but staying on my feet. I dropped to my knees in front of the toilet and hurled! My whole body convulsed, but nothing much came out. I still wasn't sure what I'd done the day before, but I could safely assume that eating wasn't a big part of it.

I put a hand against the toilet and pushed myself

up. I needed to at least rinse out my mouth or brush my teeth or— I caught sight of myself in the mirror above the sink. Very funny. There was a large black moustache drawn on my face.

I grabbed a face cloth and rubbed soap on it, and then started to scrub my face. I lathered it up good and then rinsed it away. The soap was gone. The moustache remained. This was going to take time. Time I didn't have. But it wasn't like I could show up to see the headmaster with this *thing* on my face. Especially since it looked suspiciously like *his* moustache.

CHAPTER TWO

I SAT THERE on the very uncomfortable faux-antique chair, pretending not to look at the headmaster's secretary as she perched behind her big desk just outside his office, faking work. The dark, "important" pictures on the walls—like the furniture, and everything else in the room—were just a clumsy attempt to make a statement. It was all intended to create the impression that our headmaster was a significant person, a person of substance. In truth, though, the accoutrements in our family's chauffeur's quarters were more impressive. If this office was supposed to be intimidating to students, it wasn't working on me.

I touched my upper lip with my finger. It was tender. After a quick but brutal scrubbing, the drawn-on moustache, along with a layer of skin, had gone, leaving my skin red and raw. I didn't know who had done this to me, but when I found out, they were going to pay. They thought this was so clever. I'd show them clever. No, scratch that, I'd show them mean and nasty.

On the wall behind the secretary's desk, noisily ticking away, was a big, ornate clock. I'd been sitting here for over twenty minutes. It was almost reassuring to be kept waiting. It probably meant that whatever the headmaster wanted to see me about wasn't really that important and that the two clowns who'd woken me up—who were, unbelievably, afraid of him—had misinterpreted the whole thing.

There was only one other possible explanation. Perhaps he was keeping me waiting as a form of payback, just to establish his status as the alpha dog. That was so pathetic, so juvenile. But whatever, it was fine with me. I had no desire to be the alpha dog in this place. I had no desire to even *be* in this place.

It wasn't as if this was the world's best private school. It wasn't even in the top echelon. It was simply the best school that would accept me under the circumstances and on such short notice. The "best" schools weren't so willing to consider me as a candidate for admission. I had to admit they did have some cause, but I'd never done anything really *that* serious. What self-respecting, thinking person wouldn't defy the rules from time to time? And as far as I was concerned, respect had to be earned, and none of those prissy teachers had done that. There had been graffiti and some vandalism, but it wasn't that significant and it wasn't as if restitution hadn't been given to cover the damage. And who didn't drink underage? I guess the sin was in being caught.

Apparently even schools that charge exorbitant tuition fees weren't willing to accept just anybody or any behaviour. I'd pushed beyond those limits. After numerous sanctions and suspensions, I had been "asked to leave" by several of Europe's finest institutes of high school education, and several more had been offered the distinction of having me as a student and declined. In the end, a deal was struck between this school and my father's bank account. Everybody and everything had a price, and they'd finally arrived at one they could both live with.

The new athletic centre, construction already underway, would bear our name: the Chambers Gymnasium. I don't suppose my father had to pay for all of it, but I'm sure it was a hefty percentage of the total cost. Amazing how much he was willing to shell out to keep me in school, or at least to keep me on the other side of the Atlantic, away from him. I tried my best to see the whole thing as amusing, although I don't imagine he was laughing. It was a small revenge, and maybe petty of me, but I did get enjoyment out of his having to spend a prince's ransom to keep his son away.

The ticking of the clock seemed to be getting louder. Even that was echoing painfully in my head. Just how much *had* I had to drink? I only hoped that whatever the headmaster had to say to me, he'd say it quietly. Yelling would be cruel and unusual punishment.

Now every ticking second sounded like the clock's announcing that I was being put in my place, made to wait. I got up.

"Is it going to be long?" I asked.

"I would imagine it will take as long as necessary," the secretary replied.

"Is there somebody else in there with him?"

"There is not."

"Is he on the telephone?"

She looked taken aback. As if she was so far above me or my questions that she was shocked I'd even dared to talk to her.

"I don't really know, but I certainly don't think it is any of your business to ask!" she snapped, trying to sound official, officious, important and—

We both turned at the sound of the headmaster's door opening. McWilliams stood there, filling the doorway. Of course he was in his tacky suit and a perfectly knotted school tie. He wore a serious expression on his bloated, reddish face, and his walrus moustache was practically smothering his upper lip. Even my drawn-on version looked better than his real one.

I couldn't help thinking that his reddish face matched the colour of my painfully scrubbed upper lip, but perhaps if his tie weren't so tight, he'd have a more normal complexion. I'd always wondered if he looked that way because he secretly drank. I know I'd have drunk myself into oblivion if I'd ended up like him, just trying to forget that I was stuck in this hell-hole. It would be terribly ironic if he was a closet alcoholic and was going to give me grief for drinking.

"Hold all my calls," he said to his secretary. As if any call to him could be that important.

I'd heard all the talk about what he'd done for a living before coming here, first as a teacher and then as the headmaster. Apparently he used to be some sort of special forces soldier with the British army, trained in weapons and martial arts and ... that must have been a long time ago. There wasn't much that was special about him now, and probably the only thing he could wrestle to the ground was a crumpet.

"Come," he said in his clipped English accent, motioning to me before disappearing back inside his office.

One-word commands were the norm for him, as if we were all trained collies. Or I guess soldiers under his command. There was something so irritating about somebody so obviously my inferior being in a position to give me orders and enforce them ... or at least try to enforce them.

I hesitated for a second—a small protest against being ordered about by somebody like him—and then walked ever so slowly through the open door. I wanted him to know that even if I was doing what he'd requested, it was by my own choice.

He was already sitting. His head was down, his eyes aimed at his desk, focusing on some *tremendously* important task. It was as if he was making the point that although he'd invited me in, I was of so little importance that he'd already forgotten me in the seconds that had elapsed between calling me in and my arrival.

I walked over and stood in front of his desk, beside the chair that faced him. I knew the routine well enough to know that I wasn't supposed to take a seat until I'd received that order as well. I wondered how long he'd leave me standing. I wondered even more if I should just take a seat and see his reaction. No, that would be plain stupid, and I didn't want to have to deal with the consequences if I was asked to leave this place, too ... No, wait, that wasn't going to happen. Any thought that he'd kick me out was ridiculous. The guarantee of my continued enrolment was being constructed as I stood there, and there was no way he'd risk losing that. I could expect some sort of discipline for whatever it was I'd done, but it wouldn't be more than a slap on the wrist. That way he could save face with the other students and staff, and we could all pretend that he actually had some control over me and my behaviour. As long as I didn't spill the beans as to how minor the consequence had been, nobody would be the wiser.

I had a pretty good idea about the range of punishments I might receive. After all, this wasn't the first time I'd been caught drinking. The whole place was so provincial, so puritanical, so Victorian era, so stuffy, so *British*. They all acted as though they still had an empire. That was long gone, and they should have lost the superior attitude along with it. After all, we were in Europe, and people in Europe took the occasional drink or two. It wasn't as though there was really even a drinking age here in France, and even if there was, the international schools were run like little independent fiefdoms—the residents were mostly the children of foreign diplomats, the rich and powerful, people used to not having to follow rules.

"Mr. Chambers," Mr. McWilliams began.

Everybody here was called by their last name. How military and formal and pretentious and British-boarding-school.

"Yes ... sir." Equally pretentious. All teachers here were to be addressed as "sir" or "madam" or "miss." I'd given him his "sir," but hesitated just long enough to keep him guessing about whether or not it was coming. He knew how I felt, unless he was an idiot. I'd give him the thin veneer of respect he needed to keep up his illusion of being in charge.

"Do you know why you are here?" he asked.

"Sorry, sir, I thought you'd know. I was only responding to your invitation to attend."

He looked a little thrown by my statement, but the surprise soon turned to anger. I loved the way his face got redder and redder the angrier he got. The man had a serious problem with high blood pressure. Or maybe I was right about the closet drinking. Maybe I should have brought along a bottle to share with him, or was he due for a stint in rehab?

"You are telling me that you have *no* idea why you are here?" He was trying to stay calm, but there was a slight rise in the pitch of his voice. So much for all that supposed martial arts training and staying in command of your emotions.

"No, I don't ... *sir*."

"Do you think lying will in any way diminish the gravity of the situation?" he asked.

That was obviously a rhetorical question, and I certainly was not going to answer. The secret was to never give away anything—including information—for free. Maybe he didn't even *know* about the drinking and was simply dealing with a report from one of my teachers about a late paper or a failed test—or my crooked tie.

"Are you going to deny that you were drinking?" he asked now.

Okay, at least I knew why I was here.

"You still smell of alcohol," he added.

I guess having that shot before I came to his office wasn't the brightest thing to do, but I needed a little "hair of the dog" to settle my shaking hands.

"I did use mouthwash this morning, and perhaps my aftershave has a little alcohol in it," I replied.

His face got redder. I expected his voice to rise another notch as well. His bass became a baritone and then a tenor as he got angrier. I was willing to bet that if I got him annoyed enough, I could make him sound like a counter-tenor who'd been sucking back helium.

"Are you just going to stand there, straight-faced, and boldly lie?" he snapped, his voice now another quarter octave higher, as predicted.

"I'm not lying, sir. I think aftershave does have alcohol in it, and I did use mouthwash this morning."

His face was even more flushed now—a major blood pressure rush. I couldn't help but wonder: if he had a cerebral aneurism, would I be criminally responsible?

"And you had nothing to drink. Is that what you are saying?"

"No, sir, I didn't say that. I merely said that there's an alcohol base in both my mouthwash and after-shave, and that is probably what you're smelling as alcohol this morning."

"The best lie is half the truth," he snapped. "Has anybody ever told you that?"

"No, sir, but I'm offended you would think I've been lying. I have not denied that I consumed some alcohol."

"Of course you did!"

"Respectfully," I said, the word dripping with sarcasm, "I have to disagree. You didn't ask me, ever, if I had been drinking. You simply asked if I knew why I was here, and it would have been wrong for me to suppose I knew what my headmaster was thinking. If you had asked me whether I'd been drinking, I would certainly have said yes."

"So you admit to your infraction."

"Yes ... *sir,* and I am prepared to accept my punishment."

"Are you really?"

I didn't like the way he said that. The pitch of his voice had dropped down to an almost normal level.

"Do you have any idea how much you drank?" he asked.

That sounded like another trick question. "The amount doesn't matter. The fact that I consumed any alcohol is a violation of policy."

"I think you should see the proof of your actions."

Proof? What was he going to do, show me the bottles with my fingerprints on them? Hold a little private kangaroo court with himself as judge, jury and executioner? Enough—my head was hurting and I was badly in need of another drink, and quite frankly, I was beginning to think he wasn't going to be offering me one, so I needed to get back to my room. What did he want? I'd admitted to my offence, so why not just punish me instead of making this into a piece of performance art?

"I imagine you're familiar with YouTube," he said.

"Of course I'm familiar ..." My stomach sank. This did not sound like it was going to be a good thing.

He turned his laptop around so that I could see the screen. The figures were small, but I instantly recognized the shirt on one of them—it was my shirt, with me in it. This was not going to be good at all.

He clicked on the clip and it started to roll. In a few short seconds, I realized just how bad it was. Not only was I chugging from a bottle of vodka while wearing my drawn-on imitation of his moustache, but between gulps I was insulting our school, the queen of England, his mother—in fact his whole family lineage—and his manhood. It all started to come back to me—the drinking, being egged on by my "friends." I'd been set up and I was going to get revenge on those jerks ... I just wish I'd seen it coming.

The picture froze. "I don't think we need to see any more," he said.

That was the first thing he'd said all morning that I agreed with.

"At this point, this little episode has registered, in the vernacular, close to seven thousand 'hits,'" he declared.

"It's been seen that many times?" I gasped.

"I've been told that it might in fact go 'viral,' making us *both* international laughingstocks."

"I'm so sorry."

"Are you?"

I nodded my head. I *was* sorry. Sorry that I was a laughingstock and sorry that I was going to get into more trouble than I'd imagined. What was that thing he said about half the truth being the best lie? Maybe the best thing was to get somebody else in trouble, too.

"How did that get onto the Internet?" I asked. "You know it wasn't me who did it."

"Of course it wasn't you. You were so impaired, I don't imagine that you could have tied your own shoes."

"Then who did it?" I asked.

"I would suspect that it's the same person, or persons, who notified me, by e-mail, of the existence of that piece of footage."

"Then you know who it is, right? Shouldn't they be punished? They're the ones who made us into laughingstocks."

I wasn't just thinking about what he'd do but about what *I* was going to do to *them*. By the time I finished they'd be begging to be expelled just to get away from me.

"What might or might not happen to them as a consequence of their behaviour is no business of yours. Although, quite frankly, you should know that punishing them might only make them even more celebrated amongst your classmates. Embarrassing me was one thing, but making you a joke has probably given them hero status. You are not particularly well liked, and your peers, I must say, seem to be good judges of character."

Nice—now he was taking snide shots at me.

"As for you, Mr. Chambers, I am afraid that your actions have left me with little choice," he went on.

"I'll accept my punishment," I said.

"You have no *choice* but to accept your punishment," he said. "You have one hour to gather your things."

"Gather my things ... what do you mean?"

"You are expelled."

"But—but—you can't expel me."

"I most certainly can. It is the prerogative of the headmaster to expel any student who demonstrates conduct that is contrary to the high standards of this institution, and you, sir, have certainly *shattered* those standards."

"My father ... he's not going to be happy when he finds out what you've done."

"He wasn't happy at all."

"You told him?"

"I contacted him first thing this morning."

I looked at my watch. "But it's the middle of the night in New York."

"I felt it was necessary to inform him immediately of my decision."

"I guess you didn't need a new gym that badly, then," I said.

"We do need the new facility, and it will be very much appreciated when it is opened."

"Well, good luck finding somebody else to pay for it," I snapped.

McWilliams was smiling now. It was actually creepy. "Your father has agreed to continue to fund the entire project. He thanked us for trying to provide you with an education and then apologized for your behaviour. Something, I should note, that you have not had the class to do thus far."

"You want *me* to apologize?"

"It would certainly be appropriate, given the circumstances," he said.

"Would it change the results?"

"No. You are expelled. Your father has arranged for a car to pick you up and take you to the airport."

"I'm going home?" I asked.

"I am not aware of where you are going, simply that you *are* going."

"But you still want me to apologize."

"It would be the sporting thing to do," he said.

I couldn't believe this. After giving me the death sentence, he wanted me to apologize to the man who was pulling the switch. I slowly got up from my chair.

"I hope you don't mind if I paraphrase Sir Winston Churchill," I said, gesturing to the picture of the former British prime minister that graced the wall of his office.

"Of course not."

"In that case, today I am here, expelled, and, I readily admit, still somewhat impaired," I began, "and you are a small man in a small job wearing a cheap suit. Tomorrow, I will be sober, halfway around the world, still the son and heir of a billionaire. And you will still be here, in this small job, wearing that same cheap suit. And for that, I am truly sorry … for you."

CHAPTER THREE

I WALKED ACROSS THE CAMPUS, my back straight, my pace unhurried. I wanted to convey the impression that I was leaving on my own terms and taking my own sweet time. And really, since I was the one who'd made the decision to drink and do all the other things I did, in a way I *had* chosen to leave.

There weren't many people around to see my exit—most kids were in class—but I didn't want anybody to think I was skulking away with my tail between my legs, especially not the guys who'd set me up. I was trying hard not to make eye contact with anyone, but trying even harder not to make it look like I was trying. I worked at keeping my expression neutral with a slight hint of amusement. That was the hardest. I wasn't amused. Upset, with a dash of disturbed and a side order of anger, would have been more accurate. But I didn't want to betray any of those feelings. Anger would have shown that I cared. And I didn't ... not really.

Anyway, if first impressions are important,

sometimes last impressions are even more important, and this was the last any of these people would see of me. Unless of course they ended up working for my father's company—*my* company—in the future. Then I'd get my revenge on those little toads.

Waiting for me at the curb, directly in front of the office, was my ride—my limousine. I gave a sideways glance toward McWilliams's window. I wondered if he was watching. He probably was.

The chauffeur opened the back door and I started to get in, then hesitated. I couldn't decide whether I should wave to McWilliams or blow him a kiss or flash my middle finger. Probably best to do nothing. Let him—and anybody else watching—see me getting into the big black chauffeur-driven limousine, cool, collected and calm, as if none of this fazed me. And really, why should it? This was actually a good thing.

I slumped down into the leather seat and the driver closed the door behind me. Grateful for the tinted windows, I looked out, but nobody seemed to be reacting. Evidently the show was over and I hadn't given them anything memorable. I was grateful for that, and for the fact that I could just get away. On cue, the car started moving.

The few belongings that meant anything to me had already been quickly gathered and put in the trunk of the car. It hadn't taken long to say my goodbyes, either. Maybe McWilliams was right and nobody there liked me very much. Fair enough. I didn't like anybody there *at all*.

What those jerks who'd set me up didn't realize was that they had actually done me a favour. Because of them, I got to go home, back to New York. At least until my father plotted his next move. I'd make sure the next school was at least as expensive. Who knows, maybe I could get the price set so high that he'd have to keep me around instead. No, that was wishful thinking. He had far more money than he had time for me.

I pushed the button that lowered the glass between me and the driver. Silently it glided down.

"Where are we going?" I asked.

"Nathanial International Airport—it's a private field. Your father has arranged for you to travel on his jet."

Great! Not only was it the only way to travel, but it meant that he wasn't too mad at me. If he'd been really angry, he would have made me take a commercial flight. Thank goodness I wouldn't have to be slumming it with the regular folk.

"How long before we get to the airport?" I asked.

"Less than an hour."

"And when we get there, do you know how long we'll have to wait for the plane?"

"The jet should be there when we arrive," the driver said.

That surprised me. If McWilliams had called my father first thing that morning, as he'd said, there wouldn't have been time for the plane to get here by now … would there? But technically it was a company jet, and some of the other high-ranking executives were allowed to use it if my father didn't need it. Maybe one of them was in Europe on business, and now *he'd* have to take a commercial flight back. Better him than me. Or maybe McWilliams had just gotten things confused.

Whatever. It really didn't matter, and it didn't require any more of my thought or time or energy. All that mattered was that the plane was there.

"Hopefully we'll be able to leave right away," I said.

"I'm sure they'll have to refuel and file a flight plan."

That wouldn't take too much time. All I wanted to do was get home, go to my room and lie down in my bed. I liked my bed a lot.

"I don't drive many people to the private airport," the driver said.

"It *is* a private jet."

"That's so classy," he said.

A rule of thumb was that anybody who ever said "classy" wasn't.

"Whose plane is it?" he asked.

"It's my father's jet."

"Wow, it must be nice to have a private plane."

"Yes, it is," I agreed.

"Someday I might get a chance to—"

I pushed the button and the window glided up, sealing me in the back. What was the point in continuing this conversation? He was a chauffeur and I was his passenger. All I wanted was to get on that plane.

IT WAS GOOD TO SEE the jet on the runway—a little piece of home waiting to take me home. Wait ... was it taking me home to New York, or to one of our other houses? I really didn't know where my father was. Was it possible he was in Europe, and that was why his plane was already here? It wouldn't have surprised me to learn that he was nearby and hadn't bothered to visit me at school. But that would mean he might even be in the airplane, waiting for me. I knew I had to face him, but did it have to be right now? Especially trapped together at twenty-five thousand feet for six hours? That was not the way I had it planned. I needed more time to prepare my story, and certainly a way to get some distance if it turned nasty. It wasn't like I could climb out onto the wing of the plane, and I wasn't planning on spending the entire trip locked in the bathroom.

No, come to think of it, he couldn't be on the plane. McWilliams had said he'd awakened him in the middle of the night, which would have meant he was in New York, not Europe. I was safe, at least for now.

The car came to a stop. The driver stepped out and opened my door, and then went to the trunk to remove my things.

I got out, and he pulled out the bags and went to hand them to me.

"Put them on board," I ordered, and then turned and walked toward the plane.

Standing at the top of the stairs was my father's pilot, Captain Evans, and the co-pilot, a fairly new guy. Captain Evans had been with my father longer than I'd been alive. He was old, really old, maybe even in his fifties. I had to admit that it felt a little risky to be in a plane piloted by somebody who might have a heart attack or something. Perhaps it would be wise to get to know the name of the co-pilot, at least. While a pilot wasn't really much more than a fancy chauffeur, it wasn't like we could call roadside assistance and ask to be towed if there were problems.

"Good to see you," Captain Evans said.

"It'll be even better to see home," I replied, and then paused. I needed to check. "Is my father on board?"

"He's back in New York. Knowing him, he's probably at work already."

My father was famous in the business world for working around the clock. I knew it wasn't unusual for him to be at work at three or four in the morning.

"Will he be waiting for me when the plane lands?" I asked.

"I'd be rather surprised if he was there," Captain Evans said.

That was probably the case. I was just hoping.

"Either way, we need to leave," Captain Evans said. "Please take a seat."

I wasn't going to argue with that. As Captain Evans and the co-pilot pulled up the gangway I walked down the aisle, figuring I'd sit for a while and then go and lie down for an hour or so in the stateroom.

I looked at my watch. It was just before noon—amazing how much had happened in less than four hours. I'd gone from passed out to woken up to meeting McWilliams, being expelled, packing, and driving to the airport, and now I was sitting on a jet to fly home. Busy few hours.

It was about a six-hour flight and a five-hour time difference, so if all went well, we'd be there around two in the afternoon. Assuming we were going to leave soon.

The engines started up. It wouldn't be long. Good.

Maybe it was because I hadn't eaten in God knows how long, but I was starting to feel kind of shaky and sweaty. My head was less achy now but still pretty fuzzy. The best thing for that, I'd figured out long ago, was another drink, just to take the edge off. And then I had a thought. I got up and walked over to the bar:

the only question was whether it was locked or not. I took a deep breath and pulled the handle. The door opened. It was filled with a treasure trove of alcohol—there was enough quality, quantity and variety to satisfy any and all tastes. I pushed aside a few bottles until I came to what I was looking for.

I pulled out a bottle of vodka—a *full* bottle of vodka. I broke the seal and took a little swig. I grimaced at the taste and the way it burned a passage down my gullet. I hated those snobs who talked about how they liked the taste of one brand of vodka more than another. That was like saying they liked the taste of one type of iodine better than another. You didn't drink vodka for the taste, you drank it for the effect.

I took another swig, and some of it spilled on the carpet. Oh well, not my problem. Besides, it wasn't like there wasn't more vodka where that came from. The bar was full and the door was open.

I laughed quietly to myself. Here I was being expelled from school for drinking, and nobody had had the foresight to lock the liquor cabinet on the plane sent to get me. Well, their lapse was my gain. I tipped the bottle and took a big, long drink, chugging it back like it was water.

CHAPTER FOUR

"GET UP."

"What?" I mumbled. My eyes popped open. Captain Evans was standing over me.

"Get up, we're here."

"We're in New York?"

"We've arrived at our destination," he replied.

"Oh … good … I must have fallen asleep."

"Fallen asleep inside a vodka bottle," he said, holding up the half-empty container.

"I don't think I like your attitude," I mumbled.

"Well I *know* I don't like yours."

"What did you say?"

"You heard what I said."

"Do you like your job?" I snapped. "I could fire you."

He snorted. "Your father *could* fire me. But *would* is a whole different word and a different world. Sort of like you *could* have become such an outstanding young man instead of such a major disappointment."

"I'm so sorry I disappointed you," I said, sarcasm dripping from my words.

"It's not me I'm talking about, it's your father. What a disappointment you've been to him."

I was stunned into silence.

"I remember the first time he brought you aboard the plane. You weren't more than a few months old. He couldn't stop talking about you, held you in his arms the whole flight. He just went on and on about the hopes and dreams he had for you." Captain Evans paused. "And none of them involved your being a sixteen-year-old drunk."

"I'm not a drunk!" I snapped.

"And I'm not a pilot," he said, and started to laugh.

"You think this is a joke? Wait until I tell my father what you said."

"I'm pretty certain I'll be talking to him long before you do," he said.

"It doesn't matter who speaks to him first, or what you tell him you said or didn't say. You can't lie your way out of this."

"I'm not the liar here. I'll tell him exactly what I've said—not that I haven't told him the same things about you before. But really, if our stories are different, who do you think he's going to believe, you or me?"

I wanted to say me, but even *I* didn't really believe that.

"Name *one* person who trusts you to tell the truth!" he said.

I searched my mind, trying to come up with somebody, and I couldn't. I had the urge to make someone up, just throw out a name, but I couldn't even come up with a make-believe person.

"They say love is blind, and your father has been so blind for so long. I'm just glad his eyes have finally been opened, and he's going to do what he should have done long ago."

What was that supposed to mean?

"You know," I said, "it doesn't matter who he believes or what he believes. He only has one son and there are thousands, maybe hundreds of thousands of pilots in the world. You're nothing but a glorified taxi driver."

"Even if I was a real taxi driver, that would still put me a couple of notches above you on the food chain. Now, get off *my* plane."

"It's not your plane, it's *my* father's."

"He owns it, but I'm the captain, which according to international law means it's my plane, as long as there are still passengers on board."

I jumped to my feet, and my legs almost buckled. I'd been sitting too long ... or drinking too much. I regained my balance and brushed past Captain Evans and toward the gangway.

It was brilliantly bright outside and I held my hand up to protect my eyes from the blazing sunlight. I grabbed onto the railing and started down the stairs.

It was incredibly hot—was New York having a heat wave?

I looked up through the glaring light and couldn't believe what I saw—or rather, what I *didn't* see. There were no buildings in the background, or airport terminals, or other planes, or even a runway underneath me. It was dirt and scrub bush and nothing, absolutely nothing else in sight in any direction. What was going on here? Where was I? Stunned, dazed and drunk, I tumbled down the last few steps and landed at the bottom with a painful thud! I scrambled around in the dirt and, spinning and struggling, got back to my feet.

Captain Evans and the co-pilot were standing at the top of the gangway, both of them grinning.

"I know this isn't New York, but where is it?"

"You're in Tunisia."

"Tunisia ... that's ... that's ... where exactly?"

"It's sad to see that even the most privileged education didn't teach you anything about geography. I guess you can lead a horse to water but you can't make it learn. This is northern Africa."

"But why am I here?"

"Because this is your destination. This is where you need to be."

He tossed down a backpack and I caught it, almost knocked over by the weight and momentum of it.

"What is this?"

"What you'll need to survive."

"What are you talking about?"

"There's a note in the bag from your father. It'll explain everything."

They started to pull the gangway up!

"What are you doing?" I screamed, clawing at the doorway, unable to stop it from rising.

"Wait! Wait!" I screamed, but the gangway tightly closed into the body of the plane.

This was insane, completely insane! I ran toward the front of the plane, toward the cockpit. I saw Captain Evans through the glass.

He opened up a small side window.

"You can't do this!" I screamed.

"Apparently I can."

"But what am I supposed to do?" I yelled.

"The note is in your pack. Read it."

"You can't just drop me off in the middle of … in the middle of nowhere."

"It's not nowhere," he said. "It's Tunisia, the desert."

"You can't drop me off in the desert!"

"If I had my way, I would have dropped you off from ten thousand feet *above* the desert, without a parachute!"

"You're insane if you think my father is going to let you get away with this!"

He laughed. "Who do you think thought of this? Who do you think had all this arranged?"

"My father," I mumbled. "But why would he do that?"

"Read the letter," Captain Evans said once more, gesturing behind me.

I looked back. The pack was lying in the dirt where I'd dropped it.

"I'd treat it with more respect than you usually show to people or things," he said. "Your life depends on that pack."

"My life."

I looked all around. Other than the plane, there was only sand and shrubs and rocks, and nothing … absolutely nothing else. I suddenly realized that this was life and death.

"You can't just leave me out here with nothing!"

"You have a backpack."

"You can't leave me with nothing but a backpack!"

"Oh … maybe you're right … hang on."

He disappeared from view for a second and then returned. He reached an arm through the window.

"Here," he said and tossed something at me. I caught it. It was an orange! Why would he toss me an orange?

"Eat it, jump up and down a few times, and all that vodka you've already drunk will mix together. I've heard that orange juice and vodka make a nice drink."

He began to push the window shut. I reared back

and threw the orange, and it bounced off the window.

He opened the window a bit more. "Good arm. Shame the rest of you doesn't measure up."

He slammed the window shut. Almost instantly the engines started up, and I was swallowed up by the roar. I was so close to it that I could feel the intake of air. I scrambled out of the way as the plane started forward, the tip of the wing passing just over my head.

The plane taxied down the runway. It wasn't really a runway. It was nothing but a flat, hard patch of dirt. I had the strangest urge to run after it, as if that made any sense. It continued to roll along, kicking up a trail of dust in its wake. Then it stopped and made a little turn so that it was coming back through the little dust storm it had created. It was rolling toward me. Maybe I could still stop it.

I walked right into the middle of the runway until I was standing between the two big sets of tire tracks the plane had made when it landed. If Captain Evans was going to take off, he was going to have to run me over. Leaving me was one thing, killing me might be another.

The plane kept coming, the space between us closing quickly as it gained speed. It got bigger and bigger and bigger until the sound of the engines was overwhelming. I tried to stand as tall as I could. I reached my hands above my head to look even bigger— No wait, that was what you did in the event of a bear attack. Either way, though, it would make me more visible. He did see me, didn't he?

"He's going to slow down," I said, under my breath. "He's going to stop."

He was picking up speed and he was aiming straight for me! Now he was almost on top of me, and he probably couldn't have stopped even if he'd wanted to. He was going to hit me!

My mind froze as I tried to figure out if I should go left or right, and I realized that there wasn't time to go either way! I dropped to the ground as the fuselage brushed by me. I was engulfed by a roar of sound, a rush of air blowing back my hair and then a hail of sand and gravel pummelling my face and hands.

I turned around and watched as the plane quickly gained elevation. It continued to climb, getting higher and higher and becoming smaller and smaller and smaller, until I could barely see it at all, and then ... then, it was gone.

I was lying on my belly, covered with dirt, in the middle of a makeshift runway, alone, in the middle of nowhere. No, worse, alone in a *desert* in the middle of nowhere.

I had only two thoughts: what now, and why hadn't I brought that half-full bottle of vodka with me?

CHAPTER FIVE

I GOT TO MY FEET and brushed myself off. I was covered with sand and dirt and little gritty pieces of gravel that seemed to have settled into my lungs, eyes and hair. I shook my head and dust rained down.

Slowly I walked over to the backpack and sat down on top of it. I had to think. But think about what? I couldn't even begin to work this out because it wasn't real, wasn't possible. It was like a bad joke, or a strange dream, a nightmare. If I just pinched myself, I'd wake up. Instead I started coughing, trying to free up my lungs from the cloud of dust that I'd inhaled—and generally dreams, even alcohol-induced hazes, didn't include coughing fits.

Okay, I had to settle my thoughts down. Figure it all out. Slowly I looked around, doing a three-sixty survey of my surroundings. The makeshift runway stretched out in both directions, bordered closely on either side by high dunes. They were so high that I couldn't see over them. Who knew, maybe on the other side of one of those dunes was a hotel, or a whole city?

Maybe this was all just a bad joke my father was playing on me. He was merely trying to teach me a lesson, and in a couple of minutes somebody would drive up to get me, or maybe the plane would spin around and come pick me up. This was just a bad, misguided, cruel lesson. The only question now was how I was going to react to it, and what I was going to do to turn it all to my advantage.

There seemed to be two options. I could simply act as if I'd known about the whole thing from the very beginning. Get back on the plane or climb into the car, shake my head, and then be completely nonchalant. Upside: my pride would be salvaged. Downside: it might not work in my favour right now to appear either smug or superior.

Option two: when I did get to see my dad, I could act terribly upset, scared, nearly catatonic, unable to answer questions about what happened at school because I was so traumatized by being abandoned in the desert. I could even squeeze out a few tears, fake a little hyperventilation. Upside: I could make my father feel guilty, so guilty that he'd be the one trying to make things up to me. By taking the submissive role, I could actually get the upper hand. Ah, the art of war. All's fair in love and war ... and business and family.

It was an easy choice. Besides, I *was* genuinely feeling pretty scared. All I needed now was for a plane or a jeep to appear. It was just a matter of time, I was sure. Minutes, maybe an hour at most. Okay, a couple of hours might not be out of the question, but that was the upper range.

Speaking of which, if the plane was returning, then sitting in the middle of the landing strip was probably not the best place to be. I grabbed the bag. It had some heft to it. I wondered what was inside. That might be a good way to pass the time. Some food might be in there. I was suddenly feeling hungry and thirsty. Sitting out in the open with the sun beating down, bouncing off the dunes, I felt as if I were under some sort of gigantic magnifying glass. I looked around for some shade. That didn't seem to be an option.

I was surrounded by sand dunes and a few little shrubs, their faded green the only relief from the relentless brown. It was like being at a very, very wide beach resort, without the resort, the cabanas or the poolside drink service. It was overwhelmingly dull, devoid of colour—except for one little burst of orange, the orange that I'd tossed at the plane. It was still sitting where it had fallen, at the edge of the runway. I hoped I'd at least squirted a little juice on the pilot's windscreen.

I threw the pack onto my arm and over my back, and started to walk. The sand underneath my feet was solid, which of course made sense since Captain Evans had landed a jet here. The treads of the tires were clearly visible, but the plane hadn't sunk in very far.

I bent down to pick up the orange. It seemed to have survived its impact with the glass and its subsequent plummet to the ground. I hadn't had breakfast yet, and while fruit was not high on my list, it was possibly my *only* option right now—unless there was something to eat in the pack. Or something to drink.

I slipped the orange into my pocket. Maybe later.

I shuffled my way to the side, off the runway. The position of the sun, high in the sky, was such that there was virtually no shade anywhere. The best I could do was just slump against the sand dune. At least it would be soft.

I started to settle into the sand and then had an interesting thought. What if I just went over the dune? If there *was* a resort, it might be right on the other side, or if it wasn't, maybe I could see it from up there. And if my transport should happen to come while I was off exploring, it would only make it more believable that I was scared to death, so scared that I practically ran off into the desert to my almost certain death. That would make everyone feel even worse.

I scrambled up the side of the dune, and sand avalanched down. It seemed like half of it was going into my leather loafers. Certainly my school shoes were not the best for a day at the beach or the desert.

Of course if it had been old McWilliams, he would have been in his tweed jacket and school tie, perfectly knotted. What was that saying, only mad dogs and Englishmen go out in the noonday sun?

I crested the hill. From that elevation, I could see farther. The problem was, there really wasn't much more to see. Just sand dunes leading to more sand dunes. Everything looked the same. This desert was obviously designed by somebody with no imagination or access to palettes of colour.

I slid back down the dune to the flat that formed the runway. At the bottom was a small, faded, stunted bush, somehow clinging to life against all odds. If it had been bigger, it might have provided some shade.

Sitting down, I opened up the zipper at the top of the backpack. First lucky score: a beige baseball hat just inside. I pulled it out. Hanging from the back was a sort of curtain, designed to protect the sides and back of the neck. Not particularly fashionable, but since I'd just stepped off another type of runway, I was going with function over fashion. I slipped it on, and my head and neck and eyes immediately felt some relief from the sun.

Next up was ... what was it? It had mesh and harnesses and snaps and a hose. It looked like some sort of strange bra or— No, I'd seen one of these before. Long-distance runners used them to carry water, that's what it was. Now if it was filled with water, I'd have something I could really use.

I pulled it out. The weight and the sloshing sound signalled that I'd hit pay dirt, or at least pay water. I fiddled with the little valve at the end of the hose, which was really like a long straw leading into the little compartment in the back. I put the end in my mouth and started to suck, but there was no flow. I pulled the valve and water surged into my mouth. It was warmish, but wonderful! I really wasn't much of a fan of water—it had no sugar, no caffeine and no alcohol—but this might have been the best water I'd drunk in my entire life.

I pulled the hose out of my mouth and put the whole thing down beside the pack.

Next up was a pair of running shoes. I checked. My size. Tucked inside were socks, and when I pulled them out, I realized that they were strange socks, sort of like foot gloves, with each toe having a separate little pocket to slip into. They were funny, but white and clean and certainly a better choice than my black dress socks. I slipped off my shoes and socks and put on the ones provided. They didn't feel bad at all.

Farther down was a sleeping bag. I had to give them full credit—they were playing out each little detail as if I were actually going to be spending the night in the desert. Or were they really planning to leave me out here that long ... or longer?

That thought hit me square between the eyes. Maybe this wasn't just a bad joke or a warning or a threat. Maybe I *was* being left here in the desert. If only I could talk to my father, or— Wait, Captain Evans had said there was a letter in here somewhere!

I dug down even more, pulling out a couple of shirts and two more pairs of stupid socks—and then I saw it. An envelope taped to the flap of the pack. I ripped it out and pulled out the letter. I recognized my father's handwriting.

Dear Ethan,

I know you must be terribly confused, a little scared and thinking, hoping, praying, that the plane will return. It will not. This is not an attempt to scare you straight and then swoop in to rescue you. I've done too much rescuing in the past.

There is only one way out for you now, and that's across the desert. Two hundred kilometres from where you sit is the city of Tunis. You have in this backpack the necessary tools to start your journey. But you will not be alone—I would never completely abandon you in that way.

I have been told that at the south end of the runway is a road, really not much more than a goat path. You need to follow that. Stay on the track, and do not stray. Waiting for you down that path is a man who knows the desert better than almost any man alive. He will be your guide and give you assistance to journey the rest of the way. But before you get to him, you'll have to complete the first part of the trip. You must take the first steps on your own.

I know you must think I'm a terrible person right now. Perhaps you've already thought that for a long time. I have to apologize for what I've done, and what I didn't do, over the past years. I thought that I was providing you with all the advantages, that I was giving you the best. I think it was partly my sense of guilt—for spending so much time on business and so much time away—and partly the promise I made to your mother on her deathbed that you would lack for nothing, that have caused so many of my mistakes. Not that I'm blaming her in any way. If she'd been here, by our side, none of this would have happened. She would have shown me my mistakes, helped you to understand yours, and kept us all on the right path.

In the end, all those things I gave you only became a burden that weighed you down. Your lack of disadvantage became, in fact, your biggest disadvantage. It's a lesson I've been slow to learn, but I've come to realize that in my feeble attempts to do the best for you, I've done the worst. In my attempt to give you everything, I've given you nothing. At least nothing that matters or lasts. By smoothing the road and taking out all the bumps, I have deprived you of the ability to make your own way. You need to take your own road, as we all do.

You now have two options.

You can sit there on the runway, waiting for something or someone to return, waiting for a miracle, waiting for me to somehow arrange for you to be rescued. I will not be coming. No one will be coming. If you sit and do nothing, you will die. As I write these words, I realize how cruel they sound. They are not meant to be cruel. They are meant to spur you on to go forward, to change the direction you have been on in the last few years. The path you are now on is like a slow suicide. This is my attempt to change that path.

The second option you have—the one I pray you will pursue—is to get up, put on the backpack and travel those first steps, to meet the guide and complete the journey toward your new life.

When you arrive in Tunis, the guide will take you to a law office. There, waiting for you, are documents drawn up by our lawyer. These documents provide you with a trust fund. Each year, for the next five years, you will be given a lump sum of money. This trust is sufficient to fully pay your tuition at an excellent school of your choice, plus all your living expenses.

The amount of money you will receive is dependent upon the time it takes you to reach Tunis. You have one week—seven days—if you wish to gain the maximum financial return. Each day after that will bring a ten percent reduction—the amount I deduct from my employees when they fail to make a deadline. If it takes you seventeen days, you will receive nothing. This clause was put in place to let you know that the future is now, that delaying and wasting time is what caused a great many of your problems to begin with. You must seize the day and go forward.

Along with the trust fund information, there is a plane voucher. It is an open-ended ticket that can be redeemed for whatever city you choose. I hope you will use it to come home, but I will have to accept it if you choose to go somewhere else. I have to accept it because I cannot change it. Maybe you don't even feel that you have a home to return to—but you do.

I am also aware that with this money, you could make the choice to simply finance a decadent lifestyle. It is certainly enough money to allow you to spend the next five years doing nothing but drinking, partying and wasting your time with questionable people, doing questionable things. That will be your decision.

As you can imagine, I hope you will choose the right route, but I have come to understand, belatedly and sadly, that I have limited control over the decisions you make. I have made the terrible mistake of thinking that since I control so much—so many people, so many companies and so much money—I could also control you. I cannot.

I know that what I'm doing will cause you pain, and you might want to give me pain in return—not so much for what I'm doing now, but for what I have or haven't done for so long. I already feel so much pain. I just pray that you will come back to me because you've already been gone so long.

I know you are capable of making the right choice. I only ask that you don't make a decision simply for the sake of proving me right or wrong, to make me proud, or pissed off, or sorry. This is all about you and has nothing to do with me. That was maybe the hardest lesson I had to learn. This is about you and your life.

I am so sorry for the harm I have done. None of it was ever deliberate or for lack of love. This is going to be the hardest thing you have ever done. I know it's been the hardest thing I've ever done. I know you can do it.

All my love,

Dad

I dropped the letter to the sand. This was all real. Far too real.

CHAPTER SIX

I WAS TOO STUNNED to even think straight. I desperately wanted to believe that this was just a further extension of the lesson—okay, you made your point, I get it, won't happen again—and *now* the plane would come flying back into sight. I really wanted to believe that, but I knew better. My father may not have always been a big part of my life, but when he was there, he was always truthful—at least with me. Business, of course, was a different thing, because subterfuge, misinformation and outright lying were all part of the game, but he was always truthful with the people he cared for. I guess the saying "Like father, like son" didn't always hold true.

Then I thought that maybe I'd misread the letter. Had he actually said those things? I glanced down to the ground, but the letter wasn't there anymore. I looked all around and just caught sight of the white sheet of paper flying up and over the sand dune and disappearing from sight. I could have chased it, but I doubted I could catch it, and there wasn't much point anyway. No matter how much I wished I'd misread it, I hadn't.

The letter said I had two options—although really, was dying an option?

Okay, so there was supposed to be a road at the south end of the runway, but which way was south? I figured I had a fifty-fifty chance of guessing it right, but that also meant a fifty-fifty chance of taking a long, hot walk in a northerly direction.

Wait, my father had written that I had everything I needed. What I needed was a compass. He wouldn't have asked me to go south if I didn't have a way to know which direction was south. My father would have taken care of that detail ... but he probably wasn't the person who'd packed this bag. Please, let there be a compass.

I dug deeper into the bag and started pulling everything out. Soon I had a yard-sale collection of clothing, another drinking container, a flashlight that would strap to my head and a string of some sort of flashing lights that would hang on me, a pair of sandals, some granola bars and some packages of flash-dried food—I'm sure those would taste just wonderful—and then, there it was!

I picked up the compass, and the little arrow spun around wildly before settling down and pointing in one direction: north. The clearing wasn't exactly aligned straight north to south, but it was obvious which direction I had to go. Quickly I stuffed everything back into the pack, leaving out one item—the water-filled bladder bra thing. I pulled it over my shoulder and then tried to close the clasps without success. I didn't have any experience with taking off or putting on brassieres. I guess that was one of the secondary effects of being educated in boys' schools.

I put the straw end of the hose into my mouth, released the valve and took a long sip. I didn't usually drink water that wasn't imported and sparkling and cold, but again, it was nothing short of spectacular.

I started walking down the runway, following the tracks of the plane until I got to the spot where it had lifted off and left me behind. I was now treading on virgin ground, no tracks. I looked back and noticed that my feet were barely leaving an imprint.

Up ahead a path was clearly visible. It led off from the runway and cut away through the dunes. I took a few steps and then stopped. There was a certain finality to all of this. While I was here—and here really was no place—it was as if there was still a chance they'd come back and get me. Once I left, I was clearly accepting that I had officially been abandoned and that I'd officially given up hope.

I took a deep breath and started walking ahead. There was no point in fantasizing. Staying was taking the option of dying. There'd been more than a few times in my life when I'd thought about killing somebody, but it had never been in my head to harm myself. Suicide ... now that made no sense.

The path leading away was much softer underfoot than the runway, and I was leaving tracks behind me in the sand. That had a calming effect. I could always find my way back if I needed to, like Hansel and Gretel leaving a trail of bread crumbs on their way through the forest to the gingerbread house. Right then, I'd have been very happy to see a house, or some gingerbread, or even the witch from that story.

The path curved and twisted, weaving its way between the dunes. The sun was consistently off to my right, the west. It was already slightly lower in the sky. I just didn't want it to set too soon ... I didn't want to be out here in the dark. But really, it was still afternoon, and I couldn't imagine I'd have to travel too long by myself. What had the letter said about that? Had it mentioned a time or a distance? I didn't think so. I just wished I had it so that I could check. Should I go back and try to find it? Ridiculous ... it was probably halfway across the desert by now.

I felt a sense of panic starting to rise again. I had to fight it. I told myself to calm down and be logical. I didn't have the letter, I didn't need the letter, and all that mattered was that I had to keep moving. I picked up the pace from a ramble to a march.

The path continued to cut back and forth between the dunes. I wished I could see farther ahead, but the dunes were too high. The only solution was for me to climb up one and look around.

As soon as I started up, the sand under my feet started down, shifting and sifting as I pushed against it to climb. I was making some progress but it was very slow. I dropped down on all fours, using my hands and feet to propel myself upward, and finally got to the top of the dune.

I stood up and looked all around. What I could see was simply more of the same—windswept sand dunes, brown on brown, punctuated by the occasional faded green of a shrub somehow clinging to life. The view certainly wasn't worth the price I'd paid to get up there.

I slid back down the side of the dune, a wave of sand sweeping ahead of me. I started along the path again and then hesitated—I was going in the right direction, wasn't I? It was so easy to get disoriented, to get turned around, because everything was the same in all directions. It wasn't as if there were any landmarks or signs or . . . but maybe there were a few. I looked down in the sand and found my tracks showing the way I'd come, which of course showed the way I needed to go as well.

I started moving more confidently and picked up the pace.

As I marched along I tried my best to look around. If there was anything to see, I wanted to see it. I was also starting to experience a creeping anxiety, a feeling that could almost be described as paranoia. I began to wonder if there was somebody watching me. Quickly I spun around. Nobody. Nothing. It was actually kind of disappointing.

I knew—well, at least I hoped I knew—that there was another human being close, the guide. But what if something had happened to him, or I'd made a wrong turn and I couldn't find him, or he couldn't find me? If the letter was right, I was a long way from anybody else. What a strange twist, from being worried that somebody was watching me to being worried that nobody was.

I tried to remember whether I'd ever been in a situation like this before. Had I ever been this isolated, this alone in such a desolate place, without people? Certainly we'd vacationed in some pretty exotic locations—islands in the Pacific, on safari in the wilds of Kenya—but I'd never been alone. My father was never more than a room or a tent away, and of course we were surrounded with other tourists or staff. Here, there were no other people stupid enough to think of this as a tourist destination. I was very, very alone. Or was I? I could use my phone to call my father!

I reached into my pocket for my cellphone—and it wasn't there. Had it fallen out when I was scrambling up the dune? I checked the other pocket, the place where my wallet would usually be. It was empty, too. I couldn't imagine that they'd both fallen out. They must have been taken out of my pockets before I left the plane, probably while I was passed out ... I mean, sleeping. That was annoying, to think that they'd been deliberately taken, but it did fit with the craziness of what was being done to me. And come to think of it, it wasn't like there'd be any cellphone reception out here anyway.

I couldn't call my father, but I started to rehearse in my head the conversation I'd eventually have with him. He had given me choices about what I could do with the money. I could think of some things I might do. If he thought this little lesson, this humiliation, was going to make me do what he wanted, he wasn't nearly as smart as he'd always thought he was. Ultimately there was going to be a lesson taught, but maybe I was the one who was going to teach it.

I SUCKED OUT the last little bit of water from the contraption I was carrying. Whatever more I'd need would have to come from the guide. Where was he, anyway? I had been walking for almost four hours and the sun was now so low that some of the taller dunes cast long shadows. Whenever one of those fell across the path the temperature dropped dramatically, and it was tempting to just stay there out of the sun. So far that temptation hadn't been as strong as the urge to keep moving, though. Shadows were good, but nightfall was a terrifying prospect, and I was guessing that I didn't have much more than about an hour of daylight left. I had to find this guide before dark.

Then I remembered that flashlight, the headlamp in my pack. I wouldn't be completely in the dark. Assuming it had batteries and it worked. I didn't even want to think about that. No, when the time came, I'd pull it out and it would work. I wasn't going to waste any more time worrying.

I shot a glance over to one side. Nothing but dune. What did I expect? A number of times over the past few hours, I'd have sworn I saw someone out of the corner of my eye, but there was never anybody there. Or I'd get the feeling I was walking beside something—a building or a car or a store—that turned out to be nothing more than the shadows of bushes and dunes. More paranoia, I guess. Then again, maybe I deserved to be a little paranoid, considering I'd been dropped off in the middle of a desert with night falling.

I began to wonder whether maybe the guide was secretly shadowing me. That made some sense. I started to think that my father wouldn't really have risked my life by putting me out here completely alone to stumble around out in the dunes, maybe making a wrong turn and ending up lost. I probably *was* being watched. I could just picture the guide peeking over a dune, keeping a watchful eye on me.

How strange, to feel reassured that some random guy was stalking me.

I stumbled, tried to regain my balance, but failed and fell face first into the sand. I started to get up, but stopped myself. This was the rest I needed. I pulled off the pack, set it down on the sand beside me and leaned against it.

There had been a stone in my shoe for the last ten or fifteen minutes. Sand I could handle, but the stone was getting annoying. I removed the shoe, dumped out the stone and sand ... and I had that same sense that something was lurking just outside my view. This time I wasn't going to give in to the temptation, I wasn't going to look. It was hot, I was thirsty and out of water, but I wasn't out of my mind.

And then the object that wasn't there moved!

I jerked my head to the side. Standing in the pathway was a gigantic camel! Its head was turned to the side and it was staring at me with one large, watery eye, slowly working its jaw, chewing.

I did a quick inventory of my camel knowledge: can go without water for long periods of time, known as ships of the desert and, most important for me right now, definitely vegetarian. I wouldn't have to fear it unless I was a turnip. It was harmless—no, that was wrong, they could kick, I remembered that. And didn't they like to spit? Was he chewing to work up a big wad of gob and green to spit at me?

"Go away, camel," I said in a low voice. I waved my hands in a little shooing motion, since he probably didn't understand English and I definitely didn't speak camel.

He didn't move, at least not his feet, but he did appear to be staring at me harder. Maybe he was trying to understand what I was saying. Maybe I was confusing him. Were confused animals more dangerous?

Slowly I got to my feet. "Go away," I said again, and this time my voice was louder. I was trying to sound more, well, more confident.

The camel didn't seem to pick up on the subtle nuances of my voice. Either that or he realized that he was about seven times as big as me. And then I remembered what I'd remembered on the runway, that trick of holding my hands above my head around bears. This wasn't a bear, but it was an animal, and I did want to scare it.

I lifted my arms over my head so that I would appear bigger. Still, even with my hands up high, I was shorter than him. This just made it look like I was surrendering. If he'd have been willing to lead me to water, I'd have been more than willing to be his prisoner. Or what if I captured him? I could ride him to wherever I was going! On the other hand, I didn't have a lasso or a tranquilizer gun in my pack. It was probably more realistic to hope we could call this a draw, so that both of us could get going. Now I just had to hope the camel felt the same.

"Okay, camel," I said, trying to sound friendly. "You move, and I'll go by and get on my way."

In response he shuffled a few feet forward until he was standing in the very middle of the path, directly in front of me. I wasn't leaving the path and climbing the dunes, so there was no way I could get past him now unless he moved.

Maybe if I threw something at him. But what? I felt the orange in my pocket. Not my weapon of choice, and I figured I might need it if that guide didn't show up soon.

I scanned the ground for a rock and saw nothing but sand. Perhaps I could throw a handful of that and get it in his eyes. Again, not an example of particularly bright thinking. If sand in his eyes was going to be a problem, he probably wouldn't have been living out here.

There was only one thing to do. Time to take charge. When in doubt, the best strategy was to act like you weren't afraid. Show no fear.

"Get out of my way, you stupid beast!" I yelled at the top of my lungs. I jumped forward and— He charged toward me!

I scrambled backwards, tripping and landing face first again in the sand. I flipped over quickly, just in time to see the camel run past, up and then over the sand dune, disappearing from my view.

I guess I showed *him* who was boss.

Suddenly, right beside me, a hand reached toward me out of nowhere! I jerked over to one side, crawled on all fours and then turned back around. Standing there was a man in a flowing robe with a bright blue turban wrapped around his head and face.

CHAPTER SEVEN

THE MAN JUST STOOD THERE, towering over me and my pack. He was staring right at me. Not that I could see his eyes directly. Just as his face was mostly hidden by that turban, his eyes were shielded behind a pair of darkly tinted sunglasses—Oakleys. How strange; they were very expensive, the latest fashion. Somehow that was reassuring—maybe because it was familiar, or maybe just because I could identify with somebody who had such style. On the other hand, maybe he'd *killed* somebody who had style and taken his sunglasses.

"Hello," I called out tentatively.

He didn't answer but he did take a step toward me, his hand still extended. Was he offering to help me up or did he just want to grab me? I wasn't taking any chances. I quickly got up without his assistance and backed away a couple of steps.

"Are you my guide?" I asked.

By way of an answer, he turned and walked away.

"Hey, where are you going?" I yelled, but he kept walking.

Guide or no guide, he was a human being, somebody who drank water and had to live somewhere and might have both drink and shelter to spare. Even if he was dangerous and a stranger, how much more strange and dangerous could he be than the fact of my being out here alone?

I started after him, grabbing my pack as I ran by. He was moving slowly and I quickly caught up. He gave a sideways glance but continued walking.

"I'm looking for my guide," I said. "I thought that was you."

No answer. No change in pace. No response. Was he deaf?

"I figure it must be you because who else would be out here except my guide?"

No answer.

"Stupid Arab, can't speak English," I muttered under my breath.

He suddenly stopped and turned to face me. *"Parlez-vous français?"*

"What? Oh … French … Um, *parle un petite français*."

He started speaking in mile-per-minute French, and I couldn't understand any of it. My French was pretty well limited to counting to ten and ordering food.

"No, no, *petite* French I *parle*."

He stopped talking and nodded his head. *"Sprechen Sie Deutsch?"*

"What?"

"Sprechen Sie Deutsch?"

"Oh, that's, that's German."

"*Ja, ja, das ist* German," he said. *"Sprechen Sie Deutsch?"*

"Nein," I said, offering one of the few German words I knew that didn't involve the names of automobiles.

"*Pas français, nicht Deutsch*. Arabic?"

I shook my head. "I only speak *English,*" I said, saying the words slowly and loud.

"Ah … English … interesting."

For a split second I almost didn't realize that he'd used an English word. "What is *interesting*?" I said, emphasizing the one word we seemed to have in common.

"That I'm a stupid Arab but I speak four languages, and you seem to be stumbling along in the one you *do* speak," he said.

"You speak English?" I gasped.

"Apparently with greater fluency than you do. Do you really think that by talking louder, more slowly and using hand gestures, you can transcend language?" he asked.

"But … but …"

"Concentrate. Think of the words and they'll come. You can do it."

I felt a surge of anger. "Why didn't you answer me when I spoke English?"

"What can you expect from a stupid Arab?"

"I didn't mean to offend you," I apologized.

"You didn't care about offending me or not, you just hoped I wouldn't understand that you were offending me. That's different from not meaning to offend me."

"But you are my guide, right?"

"As you surmised, that is correct."

"So you're going to take me to Tunis ... and then I can get back to civilization."

He scoffed. "Tunis is the epicentre of one of the greatest civilizations in human history, so yes, that is the plan."

"Plans can be altered," I said.

"Sometimes plans *must* be altered."

"I'm glad you agree with that. Could we talk about an altered plan?"

"We are free to talk about anything. The desert allows conversation."

I didn't know or care what the desert "allowed," but this was sounding promising.

"How about I present, as an alternative plan, that instead of walking to Tunis, we drive to Tunis?"

"Do you have a car?" he asked.

"Of course not, but we could get a car."

"Do you see any cars?" he asked. "There is no Hertz Rent-a-Car out here."

"But I'm sure that for enough money we could get a car or a Land Cruiser or something to appear."

"Like magic?" he asked.

"Money is like magic."

"Not out here. Money is useless out here," he said.

"Money is never useless. Look, I don't know what my father is paying you, but I'll pay you just as much if you can get me a drive to Tunis."

"I don't think your father would approve of that change in plans," he said.

"I don't see my father out here, so he doesn't have to know about it."

"So you would have me lie to him."

"Not lie, just not tell. It's not like you run into him on a regular basis or anything, do you?"

"I've never met your father."

"Even better."

"'Better' isn't the word I would use," he said. "But it's amazing that in the first few minutes we've been together, you have called me stupid, asked me to lie, and tried to bribe me and buy me off for a few dollars."

"It would be a lot more than a few dollars," I said.

"Aaahhh, so you aren't questioning my integrity and honesty, because you think I have neither. You are simply trying to settle on an advantageous price for those items, as if this were a business negotiation."

"I don't know about the business part, but it is a negotiation. All of life is open for negotiation," I suggested.

"I am afraid not. Some things are not negotiable. They simply are or are not."

Great, I was walking through the desert with Socrates.

"Look, all I'm trying to do is get to Tunis," I said.

"Then we have no need for negotiations. I'm going to *take* you to Tunis."

"I want to get there fast."

"Then you must walk more quickly. Simple."

"But I don't want to walk at all."

"Then you most certainly do have a problem. Tunis will not come to you. You must go to Tunis. But first we must stop for the night."

He stepped aside. In the distance there was a clearing, and in it were two small orange tents. And sitting beside them, around a small fire, were three people.

CHAPTER EIGHT

AFTER I GOT OVER the shock of realizing that we weren't alone, I watched as the outlines around the fire became real people. There appeared to be two guys and a girl—a very tall, very blond girl. She was certainly not a local. All three were young, around my age or a year or two older. Obviously I didn't know anything about them or what they'd done to get themselves tossed into this situation, but more people was better. It would mean that I wasn't alone with this guy. It was reassuring to simply have people around. Although, quite frankly, I was more comfortable when there were millions of people around.

There was also another benefit. People I knew, deserts I didn't. The more people I had around me, the more I felt in control.

They greeted us both with smiles. I guess misery really does love company.

"I want you to meet the newest member of our team," the guide said.

Is that what he was calling us, a "team"? How cute.

"Kajsa, this is Ethan."

"Pleased to meet you," she said as she smiled and extended her hand. She was very pretty and blond and tall—very Nordic, like a Viking princess. How far had her Viking ship been blown off course?

"Yes, very good to meet you, too, Kaisa," I offered.

"It's pronounced *Keesa*."

"Sorry," I said. What I wanted to say was "I don't care," but I figured an apology would stand me in better stead. No point alienating somebody I might need as an ally.

"Next up is Andy."

"Good to meet you," he said.

His expression didn't change—no smile or frown—and his eyes were hidden behind dark sunglasses, the same sunglasses the guide had. Actually all of them were wearing the same style of Oakley sunglasses.

Andy shook my hand and his grip almost hurt, it was so strong. He was tall, square-shouldered, and he had short, bristle-cut hair, like he was in the army or a cop. He pumped my arm twice and then gave me back my hand. I had the urge to check it for bruising. I made a mental note not to get this guy mad at me.

"And, finally, this is Connor."

"Hello, glad to meet you," he said.

"Me too."

His grip was more relaxed and he appeared friendly—actually kind of like a friendly member of a boy band. What had he done to get here, sung out of key?

"I'm going to leave you four to get better acquainted. I'll be back soon."

The guide turned and walked away. We all watched him scale a dune and then disappear over the top.

"At least we saw him go that time," Connor said.

I gave him a questioning look.

"He's like a ghost," he explained.

"He just appears or disappears and you don't even notice," Kajsa said.

I could certainly agree with that.

"He's a desert Ninja," she continued.

"I don't know about the Ninja part, but he's definitely special-forces trained," Andy added. "And probably martial-arts trained . . . I'd know."

Okay, so Andy clearly had some martial arts training. I underlined the mental note I'd already made about the guy.

"How long have you been out here?" I asked.

"This is our second full day," Andy replied. "We really weren't expecting anybody else to join us."

"It sort of caught me by surprise as well. Why are you all out here?"

"I'm a member of the national junior speed-skating team," Kajsa said.

"Okay ..." I was hoping she would add a bit more to that statement.

"And I'm a champion cross-country runner," Connor said. He sounded very proud.

"I'm in pre-medicine at college," Andy said. "I've ridden a bike across the States and run a couple of marathons, including Boston."

"You ran Boston!" Connor exclaimed. "What was that like?"

"Pretty amazing. Incredible crowd, so it was hard to run a great time, but I still came in at—"

"I meant what did you do to end up here?" I cut in.

"Oh," Andy said. "I guess just the usual."

"There was the application process," Kajsa said.

"I heard they had over two hundred applicants," Connor added. "And then there were the references."

"But that was no problem," Kajsa said.

"Other than deciding which references were the best," Connor said. "Then after the initial screening, there were interviews."

"*Telephone* interviews," Andy added. "We never did meet with anybody until we arrived at the Tunis airport."

"That's where we all met for the first time. Where we met Larson for the first time."

"That's his name?" I asked.

All three of them looked at me questioningly. They weren't the only ones with questions.

"You didn't know his name?" Kajsa asked.

"Not until five seconds ago. So what else did you have to do?"

"The last step, of course, was paying the fees," Connor said.

"It was pretty expensive," Andy said. "My parents lent me some of it, and I had savings from my job last summer."

"My parents helped, too," Connor said, and Kajsa nodded her head in agreement.

I guess that was one thing we had in common—our parents were picking up the costs.

"So let me see if I've got this straight. You applied, gave references, were interviewed and paid a lot of money to get here."

"Yes," Andy offered, and the other two nodded.

"Didn't you have to do the same things?" Kajsa asked.

"I'm sure my father paid money, but I didn't do any of the rest of it."

"So what did you do to get here?" Connor asked.

"Apparently I drank too much and I didn't play well with others."

"What?" Connor was voicing the surprise they all seemed to feel.

"But that doesn't make any sense," Andy said.

"I'm not claiming that *any* of this makes sense. Making sense would mean that I wasn't kidnapped and forced to come here against my will, that I wasn't made to cross some desert to get back to civilization, or—"

"Hold on," Andy said, cutting me off. "You're telling us that you don't want to be here? That you're here against your will, like a prisoner?"

"Not *like* a prisoner—*as* a prisoner, or at least a hostage."

"I don't get it," Connor said. "Your not wanting to be part of this is just way too confusing."

"It *is* confusing," I agreed. "The only thing more confusing to me is that, as far as I can see, you three actually *want* to be out here and worked your tails off to get here." I got up. "I need a drink."

"Here, let me get you some water," Kajsa offered.

"Isn't there anything else?" I asked. When faced with making friends and influencing people in new and awkward social situations, I'd always found alcohol to be my best friend. I needed to loosen up a bit, show these people what a fun guy I really was.

"We had some orange juice this morning," she said, "but that's all gone, I think."

"Affirmative, the OJ is gone," Andy stated.

Perfect. What I really wanted would have gone well with orange juice, but I was pretty sure vodka wasn't going to be one of my choices anyway.

"So do you want some water?" she asked.

"Well, if that's the best game in town," I said, "sure, bring on the water. It's a party!"

CHAPTER NINE

THE SUN SETTING threw the whole world into darkness, but breaking through the darkness were stars—millions and millions of stars—their glow punctuated by a bright, full moon. We sat around the little fire, sort of huddled on a tiny island of light in a sea of darkness. What else were we going to do? As long as I didn't stare into the fire, I was amazed by just how far I could see beyond the circle of light. Not that there was much to see, but my eyes were adjusting.

I scanned the surrounding landscape. I still had the feeling that I was being watched, and realistically, we probably were being watched. I assumed that Larson guy was sitting just out of sight, observing us like a special-forces Ninja, a peeping Tom pervert. I figured if I looked hard enough, I might be able to pick out his image before he materialized in our midst.

Kajsa stood up. "Time for a washroom break," she said.

"Again?" I asked.

She shrugged. "My father says I have a bladder the size of a walnut."

She switched on her headlamp, and the light flashed in my eyes for a second before she walked away from the fire, her way marked by the little path of light that preceded her. She slowly climbed up the dune, and then both she and the light disappeared over the top and down the other side.

I needed to go, too, but not enough to venture out there into the darkness. Sooner or later I'd have no choice, but I was hoping for later. This was the third time I'd seen her disappear and reappear, so I knew it could be done, but still, did I really want to walk into the night in the desert?

I turned around, and like magic, Larson was squatting down between the two boys. I almost did a double take. It was more than a little unnerving. On the upside, maybe his reappearance would change the conversation around the fire. All the talk lately had been about SAT scores and college applications, summer jobs and athletic accomplishments. I couldn't have cared less.

"Ethan, have you been to the washroom yet?" Larson asked.

"Many times. I've been doing it for years and years. I'm so good at it that it's been a long time since anybody has felt a need to ask me about it."

"I'm sure that's a major source of pride for your

family," he replied. "But have you gone out there?" he asked, pointing into the darkness.

"I was thinking it wouldn't be that much different here or there or back home."

"No, actually it's quite different going in the desert. You have to take the necessary precautions."

Other than something dribbling down my leg or something else getting caught in the zipper, I didn't know what precautions he could have in mind.

"Forewarned is forearmed. Could one of you gentlemen please explain the things he might want to be aware of?" Larson said.

"The most likely problem would be a camel spider," Andy said.

"Yeah, it is a bit unsettling the way they jump," Connor added. "Especially when you have your pants down around your ankles," he said with a laugh.

"And the bite is really painful," Andy said.

"Have you been bitten?" I asked.

"Not yet."

"But he's right, it is very painful. Of course pain is relative. Compared to the bite of a scorpion, it's like being kissed by a butterfly," Larson said.

"And you've had that happen, too?"

"About a dozen times," Larson said.

"Wouldn't we be better off if we were led by somebody who didn't keep getting bitten by things?" I asked.

"If you're out here long enough, it's inevitable. With the camel spider it will hurt like hell, but you won't require any treatment. With the scorpion you'll get mighty sick, you'll need medical treatment and you could end up in hospital."

For a second I thought about the trade-off: getting bitten by a scorpion versus getting brought to a hospital. I wasn't big on pain, but at least it was an option. Besides, that might turn out to be something I could use against my father—a little physical pain for some emotional blackmail.

"How would you get to a hospital from here?" I asked. "Would you go by helicopter?"

"Do you see a helicopter?" Larson asked.

"You could call one," I suggested.

"Nobody has a phone, and even if we did, there's no cell reception."

"Oh, yeah, right. Then how would you get there?"

"We'd tie the person onto a donkey or horse or camel."

"I don't see any of those around, either," I noted.

"Not here, but close at hand. There's a nomadic Bedouin encampment about ten kilometres away ... in that direction," he said, pointing off into the distance.

"And you would know that because ...?" I asked.

Larson pulled on one of his ears. "I can hear them." He turned his head slightly as though he was listening. "Can't you hear them?"

I started to listen before a smile gave away the fact that he was joking.

"I know there's an oasis that distance in that direction, and they'll be there watering and grazing their herds for the next day or so. They'd lend us an animal if we needed one. But let's just try to avoid that problem if we can."

"And how do we do that?" I asked.

"The very best thing is to watch where you're walking. Always keep an eye on the ground, especially at night when they're more likely to come up. Try to avoid bushes and rocks where they might be hiding, and make sure your tent zipper is always done up."

"I can do that," I said quietly.

"Of course those are the same pieces of advice that will keep you safe from the vipers," he said.

"Vipers … as in snakes?" I really didn't like snakes. They gave me the creeps. "Are they very big?"

He shook his head. "Small, no longer than this," he said, spreading his hands about two feet.

That thought made me feel a little better, although I certainly didn't want to be startled by one.

"And if you're bitten by a viper, it's not nearly as much fuss," Larson said.

"So they're not poisonous," I said.

"Oh, no, they're *deadly* poisonous. A bite would probably kill you within an hour or so."

"But … but … how is that not as much fuss?" I asked, incredulous.

"Well, if a scorpion bites you, we have to find a way to get you to a hospital, and that's a lot of work. If a viper bites you, we just lay you down and either the winds bury you or the jackals eat you. Either way, that's not much fuss."

Connor and Andy started laughing. Simple minds amused by simple things. I wondered just how loud they'd be laughing if one of them was stung or bitten.

Just then a light appeared over the top of the dune and Kajsa reappeared. Apparently she had survived. She slid down the dune and rejoined our little group.

All this talk about going to the washroom hadn't made my situation any better. What made it easier was that Kajsa had just blazed a trail for me. I'd just follow her tracks and be pretty sure that nothing bad was in my path.

"I'm going to try that bathroom thing," I said as I got up and turned on my headlamp.

"You know about urine, right?" Larson asked.

"Ah … I think I'm familiar with the concept … I've been peeing for a long time now."

"Again, I'm impressed, but you need to monitor your urine for quality and quantity," he said.

"What are you talking about?" Was I out here in the desert with some sort of pervert?

"It's essential that you're aware of your urine. Andy, could you please explain it to him?"

Andy nodded his head formally. I think he was fighting the urge to salute.

"The greatest danger to a desert traveller is dehydration," he began. "You need to consume sufficient water, and the best indicator of your level of hydration is demonstrated through your urination. One of the primary indications of dehydration is that the kidneys shut down and you are unable to void."

"Void?"

"To pass urine."

"Then we have no fear of me being dehydrated, because I have to pee like a racehorse, so if you'll excuse me I'll just—"

"That's only the most severe reaction," Andy added. "You need to be aware of the colour of your urine. Good urine needs to be a light-yellow colour. If it gets too yellow, or thick, you could be facing problems."

"Believe me, if my urine gets *thick,* I'll let you know. Can I go now before I wet my pants?"

"Good luck," Andy said.

I almost said something about how I was going to take a pee, not go off to war, but I didn't think he'd find the humour in that. Frankly, I wasn't sure he'd find the humour in anything.

I started off. I tried my best to move slowly, casually, completely aware that while there were only four sets of eyes within miles, they were all upon me.

I tilted my head slightly down to light a path a few feet ahead of me—a path marked by two sets of footprints, one out and one back. Kajsa's steps wove a winding route around rocks and bushes—a route I assumed was safe, or at least safer than anything I could have come up with on my own. I started up the dune, the sand cascading down almost as fast as I was moving up. Reaching the top, I stopped, out of breath, and turned and looked back.

The little fire and the four figures surrounding it were the only things I could see. In this big unknown world, they were the only things I knew at all, and I felt a reluctance to go down the far side of the dune and lose sight of them. I had the irrational thought that the moment I disappeared they would quickly gather themselves up and vanish, leaving me alone again. Technically I guess I could have just turned off my light, become invisible in the dark, and gone right there … but really, I did want a little privacy. Even if they couldn't see me, I didn't want to see them while I was relieving myself.

I skidded down the far side, taking a few steps, the flow of the sand and gravity making it much easier than the climb. I looked back over my shoulder and felt a growing sense of uneasiness. I knew they were just over the ridge, a few seconds, a scream away, but

I was once again alone. And this time I was in the dark with *spiders and scorpions and vipers … oh my!*

I chuckled to myself. Although I certainly wasn't in Kansas anymore, this didn't look like Oz, either. I couldn't recall Dorothy or Toto ever relieving themselves on the yellow brick road, but I certainly had to go. I undid my pants and quickly released a stream of liquid that drilled a little hole before vanishing into the sand. I just hoped I wasn't going to disappear the same way.

It kept flowing and I caught the stream in the light of my headlamp. It was definitely yellow, but was it too yellow? I'd never really contemplated the colour of my urine before. That was probably a good thing, a *normal* thing. What type of person would be aware of the colour of their pee? What sort of person knew if it was too yellow?

What I did know was that if quantity was good, I was potentially the Olympic champion of taking a whiz because it just kept on coming. That wasn't a surprise. I couldn't even remember when I'd drunk so much water in a day. I'd assumed that most of it had come back out as sweat, but apparently not.

When I finally finished, it was time to get back to safety. I started back to the top of the dune, carefully retracing my and Kajsa's tracks.

Just as I was about to reach the top, I had the urge to turn off my headlamp and become invisible—

maybe more than one person could magically appear out of the darkness. I reached up and then stopped myself—*spiders and scorpions and vipers.*

I stumbled over and began the descent toward the fire. My feet sank in and I slid as much as walked to the bottom. I took a spot beside the others on the mats.

"Well?" Larson asked.

"Mission accomplished," I said, giving him a big thumbs-up. "It wasn't that tricky. I wouldn't compare it to climbing Mount Everest."

"That reminds me," Connor said. "Larson, you promised us you'd tell us about the time you climbed Mount Everest."

"You climbed Mount Everest?" I asked him.

"Only once," he said. "And it's not that difficult."

"Not difficult?" Connor said. "You're joking, right?"

Larson shook his head. "At last count, close to three thousand people have done it, including a thirteen-year-old boy and a man who was legally blind. It might be the highest peak, but it isn't the most difficult."

"What mountain do you think *is* difficult?" Kajsa asked.

"Nothing seems very difficult once it's done, but if I had to choose, it would definitely be Vinson Massif."

"I've never even heard of that one," I said.

"Not surprising. It hasn't been climbed by many people because it's so remote," he said.

"Where is it?" I asked.

"Antarctica. That's what makes it so difficult. The weather conditions are very severe. It was the hardest of the seven summits."

"You climbed it seven times?"

He laughed. "I don't think anybody has done that. The seven summits are the highest mountains on each continent."

"And you've climbed them all?" I gasped.

He nodded. "But you have to remember that it's more a testament to my stamina and stubbornness than anything else."

"I'd never do that. I'm afraid of heights," Connor said.

"Me too," Larson said. "That's why I decided to climb the mountains, to help me overcome my fear."

"Wouldn't it have been easier to *not* climb them, instead?" I asked.

"Easier, yes. Better, no. You have to confront your fears if you hope to overcome them."

The other three nodded in admiration and agreement. I shook my head the other way. That was perhaps the stupidest thing I'd heard in a long time.

"I've never known anybody who's climbed the seven summits," Kajsa said.

"Again, not that unusual these days. I think there

are close to three hundred people who have done it."

"Yeah, but that's three hundred out of a world population of almost seven billion," Connor pointed out.

"So will you tell us about climbing Mount Everest or the Antarctic mountain?" Kajsa asked.

"Definitely, I'll tell you all, but not tonight. It's late and you all need some sleep."

"Can you at least answer one question first?" Connor asked. "I just wanted to know if you used oxygen when you climbed Everest."

"Yes," he said. "Some people think it's cheating, but I figure the only thing you're cheating is death. Now, time for bed. Where is Ethan going to bunk down for the night?"

"He's in with me," Connor said.

"I have to share a tent?" I blurted out.

"There are only two two-person tents," Larson said.

"But there are five of us," I said.

"I always sleep outside," Larson said. "You're welcome to do that if you want."

I knew it was already getting colder, but I'd be in a sleeping bag, and it wasn't like the canvas was going to help keep it any warmer. Besides, I wasn't worried about rain in the middle of the desert. Maybe sleeping outside wouldn't be the worst thing.

"I just need you to do up the sleeping bag very, very tightly," Larson continued.

I gave him a questioning look.

"When the temperature drops at night, cold-blooded creatures, like scorpions and vipers, look for warm places to sleep ... like the bottom of your sleeping bag. The worst thing is knowing that there's a viper in the bottom of your bag, somewhere close to your feet, and that you have to just lie there, motionless, and wait until the sun comes up. Then the temperature rises enough that it *needs* to come out," Larson said. "It would be pretty eerie to have it slowly move up your body until it came out the top, right by your face, and scurried away."

I felt a shudder go through my entire body that had nothing to do with the dropping temperature.

"It would be quite the test of one's will—overcoming your fear and mastering your emotions," Larson said. "So are you going to sleep outside tonight?"

"Just show me which tent is mine," I answered.

CHAPTER TEN

I STARTED FOR THE TENT and then did a quick turn-around and grabbed my pack. Everything I'd need for the night was in there. I picked it up—it felt very heavy now—and followed the bobbing path of my headlamp back to the tent. I dropped the pack to the ground and then bent over and undid the zipper. I climbed inside and dragged the pack—and some sand—inside the tent with me.

I was startled to see that the tent wasn't really a tent, but *half* a tent. There was a wall, the bottom half canvas and the top half mesh, that divided the little tent into two smaller mini-tents. I sort of liked that idea. It wasn't exactly a private room—actually, it wasn't a room at all, and it wasn't really private—but still, it felt good to have the illusion of privacy. I did up the outside zipper to seal me in and other things out. I didn't want to think about what could be crawling or slithering around out there. It was enough to know that with the zipper done up, they couldn't get in. I checked the zipper again, aiming my light and running my fingers along the seam, making sure it was perfectly, completely closed.

Next up I had to arrange my luxurious accommodations. I pushed the pack to one end and started to pull things out. All I really needed was my sleeping bag and the underpadding, and maybe I could use the pack itself as a pillow. I unrolled the thin foam pad and laid it out, and then put the sleeping bag on top, unzipping it. I'd just climb in and— First I had to kick off my shoes. I was amazed at how much sand spilled out of them as they flipped over.

Through the canvas I saw a light coming toward my tent. Then I heard the zipper opening and the light from Connor's headlamp flooded into the tent. He tossed in his pack and then sat down on the edge of the tent, leaving his feet and legs outside. He took off his shoes, turned them upside down and emptied them out before bringing them into the tent. He swung his legs in and then quickly did up the zipper, sealing us inside.

"It's going to be good to have a tent mate," Connor said.

His voice was friendly and cheerful, and there was a big smile on his face. He wasn't being sarcastic. He was serious.

"I thought I was going to have to spend the whole trip sleeping by myself. Andy and Kajsa don't want to share a tent with me because they say that I snore."

"Do you?"

"I don't know. I'm asleep so it's not like I would notice," he said.

Great, just what I needed.

"But I don't think I could snore that loudly or I would have woken myself up," he continued. "Probably nothing that will even bother you."

This was getting better and better.

"But if it does bother you, just wake me up," he said. "We'd better get to sleep. We're going to need our rest. Larson said we're going to do a marathon tomorrow."

"Marathon as in we're going to travel a long way, or marathon as in we're going to do forty-two kilometres?" I asked.

"Forty-two kilometres," he answered. "But don't worry, it sounds worse than it is. We did over thirty-five kilometres today, so how much harder could it be?"

The answer was seven kilometres harder, but that wasn't the answer he was looking for.

"Good night, buddy!" Connor practically sang out.

He lay down, so I couldn't see him through the mesh divider, and then he turned off his light, leaving only my headlamp to chase away the darkness. I snuggled into my sleeping bag, the light shining up on the canvas roof of the little tent. I shifted my body around, trying to find a comfortable place to settle my foam pad into the sand. I quickly realized that comfortable was not going to be on the menu tonight. But I could make it dark. I reached up and turned off my lamp, and the whole tent—the whole world—was thrown into darkness.

I TRIED TO SETTLE LOWER into the sleeping bag. I hoped to get low enough that I could wrap part of it around my head to cover my ears and try to block out the sound of Connor snoring. No, snoring wasn't the right word. I wasn't sure if it was the silence of the desert that made the whole thing seem so loud, or if he'd actually swallowed a chainsaw. Either way, it was an incredible racket.

Thinking about the other two sleeping in their tent made me a little angry and jealous, but then I realized that they were only a few metres away and the thin canvas of both tents wasn't going to insulate them from the sound. It wouldn't have been quite as bad, but it still wouldn't have been silence.

I was almost tempted to go outside to sleep. How much worse could scorpions or vipers be than this? No, scratch that thought, they could be a lot worse. There was only one possible solution.

I sat up and grabbed my headlamp, flashing it over the divide and into Connor's side of the tent. Any thought that the light would awaken him was wrong. He lay there on his back, mouth open, snoring so loudly and so strongly that I was surprised the sides of the tent weren't billowing with each burst.

"Connor," I whispered.

No response.

"Connor," I said, much louder. Still no reaction.

"Connor!" I yelled. His eyes jerked open, and then he shielded them against the glare of the light and sat bolt upright.

"What's wrong, is something wrong?" he gasped.

"No, everything is all right … sort of … I had to wake you because you were—"

"Was I snoring?" he asked, cutting me off.

I nodded my head.

"Sorry, I'll try not to."

"That would be appreciated."

I turned off the light and settled back into my sleeping bag. There was silence—wonderful, golden silence. There was no snoring, no wind, no animal sounds, no traffic in the background or airplanes overhead, no voices in the distance, no faint sound of TV or music coming through the walls or drifting down the hall. I wondered if I'd ever *heard* so much silence before. Lying in the dark in my little nylon cocoon, I could have been in space instead of sharing a tent in the desert.

Suddenly I *could* hear something, just one thing—the sound of my heart beating in my chest. I felt a rising anxiety. I sat back up and listened and looked around. I had to fight the urge to turn my light on, or wake Connor, or unzip the tent and go out and find Larson or— Connor started to snore again.

A smile came to my face. I was still in the middle of the desert, in the middle of a bizarre experience, but at least I wasn't completely alone. I lay back

ng bag again and

ffle the noise.

CHAPTER ELEVEN

CONNOR, ANDY AND KAJSA were squatting around a little mat sipping hot, sweet mint tea and scarfing down chocolate cookies and pieces of white bread slathered with marmalade as if they were starving to death. Actually, Andy ate as though he were pregnant with twins and eating for three. You'd have sworn he was having the last meal he ever expected to eat or had two hollow legs he was hoping to fill. It was like watching a well-mannered hyena feed. He was out-eating the other two combined.

Our strange breakfast featured three primary food groups: sugar, sugar and more sugar. I'd had a couple of the cookies and a cup of the tea, but I wasn't able to choke down any more than one piece of the stale bread. Probably the only thing that would have made it palatable was caviar, and I wasn't expecting anything resembling seafood.

I made a mental note—the finest beluga caviar would be part of my independence celebration when we got to Tunis. Maybe I'd even invite these jokers to join me … well, at least to *watch* me while I ate it. Giving them caviar would be like casting pearls before swine.

What I really wanted more than caviar or tea or bread or cookies was a shot of vodka. It had been almost a full day since I'd had my last drink, and I knew from experience that this could be a bit of a problem. I held my hand out and looked at it—slight shaking. I tried to stop it but I couldn't. I felt a bit shaky all over and I had a wicked headache. Maybe that was because it was still cold out, and it wasn't like I'd had a great night's sleep or—

"Are you okay?" Connor asked.

His question startled me out of my thoughts. They were all staring at me.

"Yeah, you don't look so good," Kajsa said. "You're shaking … are you cold?"

"Aren't *you* cold?" I asked, trying to deflect the attention. If there was one lesson I'd learned a long time ago, it was that you never let anyone see your weakness—never give up the upper hand.

"It's not that cold," Andy said. He was dressed in shorts and a T-shirt while everybody else was wearing a jacket.

"Maybe I'd be feeling better if I could have gotten more than a few minutes of sleep last night." That was another useful strategy: when threatened, the best defence is a good offence.

"You had trouble getting to ...?" Kajsa let the sentence trail off and then looked at Connor.

"Sorry about that," Connor said. "You should have woken me up."

"I did, and it didn't do any good at all!"

"We'll switch tent mates tonight if you want," Kajsa said. "That's only fair."

"Fair?" I said. "I'm not really looking for fair. If things were fair, I wouldn't be here to begin with."

My attention was caught by a movement—Larson had just walked into camp. He'd been gone when we woke up. I at least got some minor satisfaction out of the fact that this time I saw him coming. That was probably the best indication of how pathetic my situation was.

Wordlessly, with just a nod of his head, he came and joined the circle, squatting down between Andy and Connor.

"What does the route look like today?" Connor asked.

"There are sand dunes for the first ten kilometres or so. Then we break through to more hardscrabble, rock and salt flats."

"It'll be good to get out of the sand," Kajsa said.

"Still sand, just different sand mixed in with more rocks," Larson explained. "There are side trails branching off continually, but the main trail is fairly well defined. About twenty kilometres along is a very small oasis. Not much more than a well and a little bit of green."

"A real oasis?" I asked.

"If it has water, it's a real oasis."

"I can't wait for that," Kajsa said.

"It should be a good place to rest midday, stay out of the sun. Make sure you hydrate, and fill your water containers for the rest of the day. Once you pack up, go that way." He pointed in the direction he'd come from. "Just follow the main path until you reach the oasis."

"Aren't you walking with us today?" Kajsa asked. She sounded anxious.

"I'm going ahead. You'll catch me at some point. Just stay on the trail, stay together as a team, and everything will be fine."

He sounded calm, and that seemed to calm her. I personally didn't care. I was fine with him not being around. I'd follow the trail. The only part of "guide" I needed involved marking the trail, and he'd already done that.

"See you later today."

He grabbed a couple more cookies, stood up and walked away.

Andy got up. "Let's break camp. That oasis isn't coming to us."

They all started toward the tents. I didn't. I walked toward the mat and took a handful of cookies. The only thing I was going to put away was a little more food.

"You have to help break camp," Andy said sternly.

"I have to do nothing I don't want to do," I replied.

"But we're a team," Kajsa said.

"We're a team?" I said. "I'm not wearing any uniform. I didn't join any team."

She looked genuinely hurt. "It's just that we have to work together to reach our goal."

"*Our* goal?"

"We're all heading for Tunis," Connor said.

"Just because we're all going in the same direction doesn't mean we have the same goal."

"You eat the food, you sleep in the tent, you help to break camp," Andy said.

I popped a cookie in my mouth and slowly chewed and swallowed it. I was daring him or anybody else to do or say something.

Andy stepped forward, his eyes locked on mine. "Got it?" he asked.

"I'm going to Tunis. You three are welcome to tag along with me if you want." I grabbed one more cookie and then got up and headed toward the tent. I'd help break down the tent. I wasn't going to agree, but there was no point in disagreeing. At least not yet.

IT WAS JUST AFTER EIGHT, but the sun was already high in the sky and the heat was building on the ground. I tipped the bottle back and drained the last bit of water from the bottle. I was amazed at how much water I was drinking. At least I wouldn't have to worry about getting dehydrated … although I hadn't gone to the washroom all morning. That was the other part of it. It wasn't enough just to drink if it wasn't coming out the other end.

Up ahead, Kajsa ran off and into the dunes while the other two waited for her. She didn't have the problem I had. As she disappeared over a small hill I quickly caught up to Andy and Connor.

"How's it going?" Connor asked.

"It's going," was all I offered.

Connor looked happy and cheerful—it seemed to be his default facial expression. Andy didn't look nearly as happy. He looked annoyed, probably because they had to keep stopping for Kajsa's washroom breaks—and because it kept allowing me to catch up.

I continued walking, wondering how annoyed Andy would be now that I was in front of them. I didn't turn around to look at his expression or to let him see the smirk on my face. I wasn't going to admit it, but my need to keep up with them was greater than the fatigue in my legs or the pain in my feet. It had only been a few hours, but my feet were already starting to blister. I could feel one developing between my big toe and the next toe on my right foot. Well, at least that was the most obvious one. I was pretty sure another one was developing on the back of my left foot right where the shoe rubbed. No shock there. New shoes and a long walk through sand would be the recipe for blisters.

I didn't turn around, but I heard them coming up behind, gaining on me. Quick bathroom break, apparently. It gave me great satisfaction to stay ahead of these "great" athletes, but I knew they'd soon overtake me if I didn't start to move faster.

I set myself a challenge: to stay ahead of them for the next kilometre. If they hadn't passed me by the time I'd taken a thousand steps, I'd win. Even when they finished ahead of me at the end, I'd still know that I'd beaten them part of the way. I dug in deeper, ignoring my aching legs and focusing on the numbers—one, two, three, four.

There was a strange calmness that came with the counting. It was almost as if, even though I didn't know whether I could walk that many steps, I knew I could count that many. How many would I have to count? Okay, if there were one thousand steps to a kilometre and we were trying to do forty-two kilometres today, then all I had to do was walk forty-two thousand steps. That seemed like a lot. Okay, since I had two legs, I only had to walk twenty-one thousand steps per leg. I'd start counting every second step as a "one" until I reached the goal.

I kept counting, but at the same time I tried to figure out how far we'd already gone today. I didn't need to do twenty-one thousand more steps because we'd certainly covered ten or twelve kilometres already.

I reached a count of one hundred steps on my right leg and put down my baby finger on my right hand, curling the rest up, and started to count from one again. That was one fifth of a kilometre, twenty percent, and they hadn't caught me. I wanted to look back and see if they were gaining, but I didn't want to risk letting them know that we were in a race. Besides, I'd found a rhythm and I didn't want to break that by breaking my stride. I'd just keep moving forward, step by step, number by number, counting them off, adding them up, staying ahead.

I PUT DOWN the last finger on my left hand. That was one thousand steps with my right foot—two kilometres—and I was still ahead of them. True, I could hear them now, but they still hadn't caught up to me. It had been over a year since I'd done anything more physical than walking to class, but it was starting to feel like the benefits of all those years playing soccer and rugby hadn't completely drained from my system. I'd also run some cross-country—I'd been on the team at one school before I got expelled—so I knew I had some kick to my legs.

I also knew that I couldn't keep this pace up all day, but then again, I didn't have to. We were going to stop at that oasis, and it couldn't be more than seven or eight or nine kilometres away. It would be amazing to be sitting there, my feet in a pool of cool water, when they walked in.

I caught sight of movement on the ground. When I looked down at my feet, I did a quick little jog and jump to avoid stepping on a line of ants marching across the path.

"Get out of the way before you get hurt," I mumbled at them as I looked back. "They may not step over you!"

Looking farther back, I saw the three of them, closer than I thought, looking at me strangely. I could only hope they hadn't heard me, but they probably couldn't have missed my little dance step.

I spun back around, my eyes down and to the front. Why did I care what they saw or thought? They weren't that important now, so in a few days they'd be almost beyond trivial. I'd be shocked if I even remembered any of their names a month from now. Okay, maybe I'd remember Kajsa, but I was positive I wouldn't remember how to say it right, and I wouldn't even want to hazard a guess as to how you spelled something that strange.

Actually, come to think of it, once I reached Tunis and got my money, I was going to have such a long party that I wondered if I'd remember how to spell *my* name in a month.

I held up a hand. The shaking had almost gone completely. I'd heard about drying out, and I'd certainly been doing that. Dried out, dried up, baked, oven-roasted and practically microwaved.

I heard steps coming up from behind me. I turned around slightly and saw Kajsa jogging forward, leaving the other two behind. Had she figured out the little game I was playing, or was she running because she thought there was a washroom up ahead?

She fell in beside me, panting, sweat rolling down her face, her cheeks bright red. Shockingly, she was still awfully good-looking despite it all.

"That was sweet of you," she said.

"What was sweet of me?"

"The ants."

"You saw the … what ants?" I asked, playing innocent.

"I saw you make sure you didn't step on them."

"How could you see … what are you talking about?"

"I saw you jump and wondered if you'd seen a viper or scorpion," she said. "And then when we got close to the spot where you'd jumped, I saw your tracks and the army of ants. You didn't want to step on them. That was so *sweet* of you!"

"I don't know what you're talking about."

"Okay, deny it if you want," she said. "But I still know."

I wasn't sure if I liked her thinking of me as "sweet." I mean, maybe it gave me an advantage if it meant she underestimated me, and maybe it would even make the other guys a bit jealous, which might be kind of fun. But now she kind of had something on me—I was a big softie. Time to get the upper hand again.

I let out a big sigh. "I'm surprised you haven't gone to the washroom in a while."

"I'm trying to hold it in."

"That must be hard with all the water you're drinking. You must feel like your bladder is practically bursting."

"I'm fine," she said.

"That's nice to hear. Do you want a drink?"

I held the bottle in front of her and swirled it around.

"I think I'm going to have to stop soon myself," I said. "Doesn't the sound of that water sloshing around in there make you think you need to—?"

"Excuse me," she said.

She took a sharp left turn and headed into the dunes to relieve herself once more. This was all way too easy.

I STUMBLED AS I TRIPPED over a stone sticking out of the sand. My stride broke, my rhythm was gone. But it didn't matter so much because the numbers I was counting had stopped when the others had passed me. They were about to disappear over a little rise, and the only thing keeping me going was a desperate need to try to keep them in sight. Why didn't they just stop? Wasn't Kajsa due for another washroom break soon? Shouldn't we have reached the oasis already? Were we even going in the right direction, or was I simply following three people who were lost ... which, of course, meant that I was lost, too?

They had reached the crest, and I could now see less of them with each step forward. It was as if they were being swallowed up by the desert, inch by inch, starting at the feet. Actually, it was more as if they were being worn down or were melting into the ground. I watched, fascinated, until their legs disappeared, then their upper bodies dissolved and finally three bobbing heads vanished and I was alone.

Despite the rubbery feeling in my legs and the pain in my feet, I stumbled forward a little faster. Being alone in the desert was even worse than simply being in the desert. I just wished I had something to give me a boost, if not a real drink, then at least an espresso or a Red Bull or— I remembered that I still had that orange stuffed into my pocket. I pulled it out.

It was fairly big and firm, and I could almost taste the juice inside. If I'd had any saliva in it, my mouth would probably have watered. I held it up. The way the sun caught it, the bright orange practically glowed. It certainly stood out in sharp contrast to the colour—really the lack of colour—that enveloped me. Somehow that lack of colour seemed as oppressive as the heat. I had this bizarre thought that I could keep the peel after I'd eaten the orange, sort of like how a big-game hunter keeps the head or skin or antlers of his kill.

"Well, orange, sorry to have to do this to you."

Okay, I was now talking to an orange. Even worse, I was apologizing to an orange. I guess I wasn't totally crazy as long as I didn't think it was talking to me. I held it up to my ear. Silence. It didn't say a word. Very brave, not begging for its life. I had to admire its courage as much as I admired its colour.

Thinking back, my only regret was that my aim had been a little off when I tossed it at the plane. It would have been amazing to have hit Captain Evans with it—smack him square in the face and wipe that smug look right off it.

Then I had the strangest thought. It wasn't too late. I was going to cross the desert, get back home and give him back his orange. I wasn't going to toss it at him. Instead I was going to walk right up and say, "Here, you dropped this," and hand it back to him. That would be perfect.

"Okay, orange, you have a reprieve. The governor has repealed your death sentence ... you get that? ...

re*pealed* … a little play on words … pretty clever, don't you think?"

He didn't answer. Apparently he *didn't* think it was that clever, which undoubtedly showed he was a cultured and refined orange not fond of puns, which were, of course, the lowest form of humour. I was grateful. If this orange was going to be my companion for the next while, it was good not to have a common fruit as my friend.

I tossed the orange slightly up into the air, catching it.

"Now all you need is a name. What should I call you?"

Again, no response. Obviously he did not have a clear preference.

"Well … we're in a foreign and strange place, so I think you need a foreign name. Orange won't do … wait … perhaps you're like the French Foreign Legion walking across the desert. I'll call you L'Orange … no, that's too simple … L'Orange of Tunisia! You'll be like the citrus version of Lawrence of Arabia! It is an honour to meet you, Monsieur L'Orange of Tunisia!"

I crested the hill and practically bounced into Andy and Connor, who were standing there in the middle of the trail! They both gave me strange looks, as though they'd heard me talking to myself.

"I was singing," I said. "I'm just so happy, I was singing to pass the time."

They both nodded, although neither looked convinced. I tucked L'Orange back into my pocket.

I was going to ask where Kajsa was, but that was too obvious. She came trotting out of the scrub brush to the left. No sooner had she arrived than we all started walking again, me just behind them.

"Are you drinking enough water?" Connor asked, looking over his shoulder.

"Drinking so much my teeth are practically floating away."

"It's not your teeth you should worry about, but rather your kidneys," he said.

"I don't think I'm the one who should be worried about my kidneys." I pointed at Kajsa.

"It's my bladder that's the size of a walnut, not my kidneys," she said. Then she laughed, but it was anxious laughter. There was something there that made her nervous. That worked for me—a chance to widen the chink in her armour, start messing with her head.

"You should have a doctor check things out," I said.

"I have had it looked at," she said. "My family doctor did some tests."

"Family doctor? Maybe you should have had a specialist. You just can't be too careful. Something for you to consider when you get back home."

I looked over at her. Anxiety had given way to full-fledged worry. Now to push it to a higher level. Let's go for panic.

"If it was me, I'd take care of it right away. First thing, as soon as I got back. Maybe you can contact your parents and have them arrange it. You don't want to waste any more time. Sometimes a few days is the difference between life and ..." I let the sentence trail off.

She had to be smart enough to finish that sentence.

"But I'm sure it's nothing ... really," I continued, trying to sound sympathetic instead of sinister. But I had definitely thrown her off her game.

I was enjoying this. Actually I was enjoying just talking to somebody, anybody, even these three. Not that L'Orange hadn't been a good listener.

The two boys were starting to pull away a little, and they were pulling her along with them. I didn't want to speed up—I wasn't sure if I *could* speed up—but I didn't want to be alone again right now, either.

"Could I ask you three something?" That was a rhetorical question, since I was going to ask it anyway.

"Of course," Connor said.

"Affirmative," Andy added.

I wanted to ask *him* if he'd been obsessed with G.I. Joe when he was younger, but I had something else in mind.

"I just wanted to know why you all decided to come out here and do this."

"Probably slightly different for each of us," Connor said.

"But probably the same for all of us as well," Kajsa put in.

"And?"

"It has to do with the challenge, at least it does for me," Connor said.

"Me too," Kajsa agreed. "It's the thrill of attempting something difficult and accomplishing it!"

"Exactly," Connor exclaimed.

"And for you?" I asked Andy.

"Simple. It's important to push yourself to the limit. By crossing the desert, we prove we can overcome, we can survive. To survive is to succeed. It's a sense of pride."

I was impressed with the quantity of words, if not the quality. That was about the longest sentence I'd heard him string together, even if what he said made about as much sense as stringing together bumper stickers or fortune cookies.

"So when we get across the desert, you'll be proud of yourselves," I said.

"Well ... yeah, I guess," Connor said.

"That is so strange."

"What's strange?" he asked.

"You're going to feel proud that you did something that didn't need to be done in the first place, something that has absolutely *no* value."

"Accomplishment has value," Andy stated. "Not *everybody* can walk across a desert."

"Not everybody would *want* to walk across a desert. Let's say instead that you ate thirty-five hamburgers in thirty minutes and won a food-eating contest. Would you feel proud of that accomplishment?"

"Apples and oranges," Andy said.

"Let's just stick to the food group that I'm talking about. Are you saying that doing anything other people can't do is an accomplishment?"

"Well, not anything," Connor said. "But this is really, *really* difficult."

"I think eating thirty-five hamburgers would be really, *really* difficult."

"I think Andy could handle it," Connor said, and Kajsa laughed.

"I've never eaten thirty-five ... at least at one sitting," Andy agreed, and he gave a slight smile. "But whatever goal I set, I reach. Period."

"Determination is what sets apart great people," Kajsa said.

"So you think Andy is great?" I asked.

"No! I mean, someday he might be ... I mean, I think he *will* be."

"And crossing the desert is part of that?" I questioned.

"Part of it," she said.

"Great people. So who would you consider to be a great person?" I asked.

"Martin Luther King, Gandhi, Mother Teresa and Nelson Mandela," Kajsa said without hesitation.

"Those people, of course," Connor agreed. "But also people like Jackie Robinson, Muhammad Ali and Roger Bannister."

"The first two I know, but who is Bannister?"

"He was the first person to break the four-minute mile. He's one of my heroes."

"I see, and Andy, who do you want to put on that list?" I asked.

"Henry Ford, Thomas Edison and Bill Gates."

One picked humanitarians; the other, sports figures; and the third, people who made a lot of money from their inventiveness. My father would have approved of those last choices for sure.

"Those are amazing people, no question, but as far as I can tell, none of them ever crossed a desert."

"What?" Connor asked.

"They all did amazing things, but none of them, if I'm not mistaken, ever walked across a desert. Maybe the key is if you want to be great, you should spend your time doing something important instead of walking across a desert. Come to think of it, I can't think of even *one* great person in the history of the planet who ever walked across a desert. Can any of you name anybody?"

"Um ... not really," Connor said.

"Moses," Andy said.

"Moses?"

"He was a great person. He led his people across the desert to the promised land."

"He's got you there, Ethan!" Connor exclaimed.

"Do you think so?" I asked.

"I wouldn't have mentioned him if I didn't think so," Andy said.

"If I recall the story, Moses spent forty years in the desert, sort of wandering around until finally he died *before* they reached the promised land. So if you think about it, not only did he not cross the desert, he died in the desert."

They looked at Andy for a reaction.

"At least he died trying. That says something about the man," he said.

"Yeah, it says he *died*. Is that really the role model you're going for?"

We walked along in silence for a while. I figured I'd won our little war of words.

"So if you don't see the point in all this, why are you here?" Kajsa asked.

"First off, you all know that I'm here against my will, and that I'm walking for one simple, pure reason. Money."

"Money is a pure reason?"

"More pure than anything else I know."

"And if you do manage to cross the desert—"

"Oh, I *will* cross the desert. There's too much money at stake for me not to."

"Okay, are you telling me that *when* you cross the desert, you're not going to feel just a little bit proud?" Connor asked.

"I will," I agreed. "I'll be proud that I got the money."

Kajsa slowed down and came to a stop, and the three of us did the same.

"I'm afraid I have to ... you know."

"I'll see you three in Tunis." I started walking again.

CHAPTER TWELVE

THE SUN WAS LOW ENOUGH in the sky that we were now in the shadows cast by the dunes. I was so grateful for the shade, so grateful that the sun was going to set. I'd never looked forward to dusk so much before. My mind drifted back to that little oasis—really just a small puddle of blue with a few dashes of green. Larson has said we had to travel farther that day; otherwise we could have stayed there. It wasn't much, but compared to the rest of the landscape, it was a little piece of heaven. Walking away from that had been the hardest thing I'd had to do so far.

"You should come and get some food," Larson said.

He offered me his hand. Slowly, unaided, I got to my feet and limped away, leaving him behind.

"Feet or legs?" he asked as he trailed after me.

"What do you mean?"

"Is it mainly your feet that hurt or your legs?"

"Both, but mainly my feet. Blisters."

"Are they bad?" he asked.

"Is there such a thing as a *good* blister?"

"Some are worse than others."

I came up to where the other three were sitting, starting to eat. More white bread was being passed around. In the middle was a steaming pot of something. Larson lifted up the lid and started ladling it out into waiting bowls.

"Grab a bowl," he said.

"What is it?" I asked.

"Does it matter?"

I shook my head. "Just wondering."

"Try it." He offered me a bowl and a spoon.

For a half second I thought about refusing it, the way I'd refused his hand in getting up, but that would have hurt nobody but me. I took it and shovelled down a big spoonful.

"This is good."

"When you're hungry enough, everything is good. Come and join us." He patted the mat between him and Kajsa. She moved slightly to the side and smiled.

Carefully I settled in, my knees almost buckling under me as I sat down.

"So I wanted to let you know how well you all did today, especially you, Ethan," Larson said.

"Why me? We all walked the same distance."

"But the others are all endurance athletes who followed a specific training plan for months prior to coming here."

"That's right," Connor said. "Since you didn't know anything about being out here, you couldn't have done any training."

I nodded my head in agreement, although I felt like saying, "Way to go, genius."

"Then you're doing incredibly well," Kajsa said. "You should feel proud!"

"Not yet. Still no money, so still no pride." I paused. "I guess in some ways, all that training you three did wasn't really necessary."

"We won't know about that until we reach Tunis," Larson said. "But first things first: let me look at your feet."

"First you want to know about my urine, and now you want to look at my feet. You're into some pretty kinky stuff," I said, trying to sound funny, but just sounding sad.

"Urine and feet are in the same category. Both involve keeping you moving forward. Take off your shoes and let me look at your blisters."

"What good will that do?" I asked.

"I can take care of them. Make sure they don't get infected. That would do a lot of good," Larson said.

"Really?"

"It helped with my feet," Kajsa said.

"You got blisters?"

"We all got blisters the first day," she said.

I wanted to say something about Andy's skin being too tough to blister, but thought I'd keep that to myself.

"If he doesn't want his feet looked at, you can fix up mine," Andy said.

"You all eat and I'll get the first-aid kit. Best we take care of this before it gets dark."

He got up, and all three of them started taking off their shoes and peeling off their socks.

I put down my bowl and did the same. As soon as my socks were off, the damage was pretty obvious. In spite of the fancy socks with individual toes, there were large, puffy red balloons between both of my big toes and the middle toes.

"That is nasty looking," Connor said.

"Way worse than my little blisters," Kajsa said.

I couldn't even see any blisters on her feet. I guess they were hidden underneath the little bandage on the back of her foot.

"Maybe that's one of the advantages of training," Andy said.

Larson returned with the first-aid kit. "Blisters are not bad," he offered. He pulled a small knife out of the kit. "I'm going to slice them open to allow them to drain. It won't hurt ... well, not nearly as much as the blisters do."

"Whatever. Do what you need to do."

He took the tip of the knife and made an incision

along the length of the first blister. It oozed out clear liquid.

"Blisters are just the way your body protects itself. It builds a cushion to protect you. And then that blister, once it's been burst, like this, becomes a callus, and calluses are stronger, tougher than the original skin," he explained.

I chuckled. "Just what I need, a little philosophy class."

"What do you mean?" he asked, trying to sound innocent.

"I get it. I understand the point you're trying to make."

"And what point is that?"

"You're saying that getting hurt makes you stronger and tougher. And because I've been hurt, that should make me tougher … right?" I scoffed. "You're trying to say that the difficulty of completing this trip will make me tougher and stronger."

"I was talking about your *feet,*" he said. "Blisters becoming calluses. That's all I was talking about. Really." He paused. "But what you're saying does make sense. You're pretty insightful."

I didn't feel insightful. I just felt stupid.

He took the knife and made an incision on the second blister, and it burst open, practically spraying out clear liquid.

"But if you want philosophy, I'll give you the most

important piece of philosophy I know. *Moderation in all things,*" Larson said.

"That sounds like something Aristotle would say," Andy remarked. "He taught the doctrine of the mean."

"Very impressive," Larson said.

I wasn't impressed so much as nauseated.

"I took a course in philosophy because I thought it would look good when I applied to medical school," Andy added.

"Philosophy is useful in all walks of life," Larson said. He held up a little bottle. "Now this might hurt a little."

"What is it?"

"Iodine. It will stop the blisters from getting infected and dry them up so the calluses can form."

He uncapped the bottle. It had a little brushlike applicator, and with it he began painting my blisters. The orange liquid stung. I tried not to show any reaction.

"Aristotle believed in a golden mean that is the desirable middle point between two extremes," Andy continued. "Courage is a desirable trait, but too much courage produces reckless behaviour, whereas too little results in cowardice."

I glanced over at Andy, who was looking sickly smug. Okay, we all got it, you know, who Aristotle was. Was he hoping for a cookie?

"Although that specific quote was actually *not* from Aristotle," Larson put in, and Andy looked a little deflated, which, I've got to say, made me pretty happy.

"It's attributed to the ancient Roman playwright Terence, who was alive about two hundred years after the time of Aristotle, so perhaps he was influenced by him."

"He probably was," Andy said, looking to save face. "But it is a common belief. Buddhists believe in the middle way, while Confucian thought extols the moderate. And of course, carved on the Temple of Delphi are three simple words: *Excess in Nothing*."

"That's all pretty amazing," I said, "but has anybody thought about the fact that there's nothing moderate, no middle way, in walking across the desert?"

"You're right, and that's why I personally believe in the second part of the saying: *Moderation in all things, including moderation*."

"So what exactly does that mean?" I asked.

"It means that if you're moderate in all things, that would be extreme or excess moderation. So you have to have some things you're *not* moderate about, one or two things in which you're extreme, about which you're passionate."

"And that's why we're here," Connor said. "Because we're passionate about pushing ourselves."

"That's why *you four* are here. That's not why I'm here."

"But you must be passionate about something, right?" Kajsa said.

"Um … sure … of course … everybody is." I paused. "I'm passionate about getting out of the desert and making it to Tunis."

"Nothing else?" she asked.

"Nothing else that I want to talk about."

"There, all done," Larson said. "You're probably going to lose a couple of those toenails."

I looked down at my feet. They were orange all around the two toes. I couldn't wait to show L'Orange.

"I used to have a lot of problems with my toenails. I'd lose them all the time," Larson said.

"But you don't now, right?" Connor asked.

"You can't lose what you don't have. I had them removed."

"You *what*?" I exclaimed.

"I had them surgically removed. I have no toenails."

"But that … that's … so *not* moderate."

He laughed. "It is a little excessive, and in hindsight, I wish I hadn't done it."

"Enough about your toenails," Kajsa asked. "How about if you tell us a story."

He got up. "My stories aren't that exciting."

"How can climbing Mount Everest or running across the Sahara Desert not be exciting?" Connor asked.

"You ran across the Sahara?"

"Not all at once."

"I don't know what that means. Did you do it in stages?" I asked.

"In a way. There were three of us, and we started in the west at the Atlantic Ocean and ran until we reached the Red Sea. It took us over one hundred and fifteen days."

"In a row?"

He nodded.

"They averaged over seventy-five kilometres a day for those days," Connor said.

"Come on, that's impossible. Nobody can run seventy-five kilometres a day … any day … let alone for a hundred and fifteen days in a row, across a desert," I said.

"It does sound impossible, but we made it possible," Larson said. "Still, it's not much of a story. We just ran, step after step, day after day. Very boring. How about if I tell you about the very first marathon? Does anybody know that story?"

I chuckled. "Is there anybody who *doesn't* know that story?"

Connor, Kajsa and Andy all nodded their heads knowingly.

"Okay, what story do you four know?" Larson asked.

"Well, some guy in ancient Greece—" I began.

"His name was Pheidippides and he was from the city-state of Athens," Andy said.

"Isn't Athens in Greece?" I demanded.

"Well, yes, now it is, but technically—"

"Technically, *I* was telling the story," I said. "So he and the other Greeks won a battle against some enemies—"

"Persians," Andy interjected. "Sorry."

"So they beat their *enemies* at a place called Marathon, and Pheidippides was so proud that he ran all the way back to Athens, a distance of twenty-six miles, to tell them that they'd won the battle. And right after he told them, he was so exhausted that he died. The end."

"Does anybody else have anything to add?" Larson asked.

"Wasn't the Persian army a lot bigger?" Connor asked.

"They had somewhere between six and ten times as many men, plus six hundred ships and cavalry," Larson said.

"Couldn't he have borrowed a horse and ridden to Athens?" I asked.

"He could have, but it would have been slower," Larson said. "In a race of that length, men almost always outrun horses."

"You're joking, right?"

"He's not," Kajsa said. "They still have races like

that, and sometimes a man wins and sometimes a horse wins."

"If he'd taken a horse, at least he wouldn't have died," I countered.

"Point taken," Larson said. "But let me tell the whole story. As Andy has said, Greece was divided into city-states, with Athens and Sparta being the two most prominent. Both states knew that the plan of the Persian Empire was to take each state, one after the other, so that it would be in the best interests of all to work as one. That Greek guy, Pheidippides, was a military messenger. He ran to deliver a message to Sparta, one hundred and forty miles away, asking them to join in with the Athenians. He then ran back, covering another hundred and forty miles, to say that the Spartans would come and join in, but not for another week. He ran more than a marathon every day for six days."

"Even more impressive," Kajsa said.

"Then, upon his return, he joined in with the Athenian army that attacked the Persians. The battle lasted a full day, during which thousands of Persians were killed and the rest were driven back to their ships and sailed away."

"And *that's* when he ran to tell them about the victory," I said.

"No, that's when he ran to warn the Athenians that the Persian fleet was coming," Larson said. "The

Persian forces still vastly outnumbered the Greek forces, and they were going to attack the now largely undefended city of Athens."

"So he wasn't just running to brag," Connor said.

"Far from it. He ran to warn, to give hope and to tell them that the entire Greek army was running back, in full armour, to do battle with the Persians as they landed."

"The entire army?" Andy asked.

"It took Pheidippides three hours. Within six hours, the majority of the Athenian army, in full armour, carrying their weapons, had arrived on the beach and were there waiting when the Persian fleet arrived."

Andy laughed. "Those Persians must have been surprised!" I could see why Andy would like this story. I could see why Andy would have made a great Greek soldier.

"The Persians were so astonished that they believed the Greeks were almost supernatural. Instead of invading, they simply sailed off."

"What a military victory," Andy said.

"It was far more than that. It allowed the Greek cultures to flourish and spread throughout Europe. Because of that victory, we have democracy, freedom, philosophy."

"Bumper stickers," I mumbled under my breath.

"And that's the full story of the first marathon and a Greek guy named Pheidippides."

"A *hero* named Pheidippides," Andy said.

"That is so inspirational," Connor said.

I stood up. "It certainly inspired me."

"That's nice to hear."

"It inspired me to know that if we ever win a battle out here, I'm sending Andy to tell people about it."

Andy looked pleased—and confident. He probably could have run a full marathon in armour carrying a weapon.

"And me, I'm going to wait a few hours, maybe rent a camel, take my time and make sure I live to see the end."

"Or you might just live to see the destruction of your city at the hands of the victorious enemy. Regardless, we might want to head to our tents now," Larson said. "We have to turn our attention to the weather. There's a storm coming tonight. A big storm."

I looked around. Everybody looked around.

"How can you tell?" I finally asked.

"I can smell it ... I can feel it. The winds are shifting and building."

I couldn't smell or feel anything.

"We have to put everything inside the tents and make sure they're staked down. It's going to be a bad one."

I got up and walked away from the group. Out of earshot, I slowly pulled L'Orange out of my pocket.

"Idiots," I said softly. "Only a bunch of idiots would think a Greek idiot running himself to death was anything more than idiotic. It's sad when the second sanest thing here is an orange."

L'Orange didn't answer. He didn't need to answer, which of course meant that he agreed completely.

CHAPTER THIRTEEN

IT SOUNDED LIKE A FREIGHT TRAIN passing right by the tent, or more correctly, passing right *through* the tent. It wasn't just the wind, which sounded like a hurricane, but the sand being driven against the tent, and the tent wildly beating like a living animal trying desperately to fly away. It wasn't reassuring to know that the only things stopping it were a few small stakes in the shifting sand and our body weight. Down at my side was my headlamp. I had the light on low so that it gave a glow to the tent. It was comforting to be in a little puddle of light in the middle of this sea of a storm.

The tent was sealed up, the screen zipped shut and the flap tied down, but the winds were so strong that the sand was being driven through the mesh. It had started out as a fine film of grit, almost like baby powder, but it kept on accumulating until it was now piled on the floor and layered on everything inside. I kept brushing it off my sleeping bag, but it was a useless exercise. It was everywhere, including on my face and arms, and in the light of my headlamp I could see it, floating through the air.

I kept one hand on the side of the tent, trying to steady it, sort of the way you'd place a hand on a horse to calm it down when it was spooked or scared. Of course the tent wasn't alive, and it was me who needed to be calmed down.

The wind was blowing directly toward my side of the tent, and it had started to undermine the ground—the sand—underneath so much that I was tilting into a ditch the length of the tent. I wondered how long it would be before the stakes on that side were completely uncovered and lost their grip on the ground, and the whole tent would fly free. Something else I didn't want to think about.

"Are you still awake?" Connor called over the divide.

"I didn't think anything could be louder than your snoring, but I was wrong."

"Thanks for offering to share the tent with me again tonight."

"No problem."

It wasn't a selfless act. As the storm gathered, I'd quickly realized that the sound of the wind would be louder than his snoring. And by being with him two nights in a row, I could probably be free of him another two nights.

"Do you think it's going to break before the morning?" Connor asked.

"You'd have to go out and ask Larson that one."

"I can't believe he's sleeping out there. We could have made space for him in here."

"Where?" I questioned.

"We all could have squeezed in."

"He said he'd be okay out there, and you pretty well have to believe him."

"I guess we should just try to get to sleep," Connor suggested.

"Easier said than done."

I turned off the light and the tent was thrown into complete and utter darkness. The storm had obliterated any light from the stars or moon above. And in the pitch black, it was as though my other senses were thrown into overdrive. It wasn't just the sounds—the roar of the wind and the flapping of the tent—but that I could feel the grit against my skin and going into my lungs with each breath. I could taste it in my mouth. I had to try to take my mind off the storm.

My head bounced from one thought to another—being kicked off the plane, my father's letter, meeting Larson, the insanity of the walk, the intensity of the heat, my blisters and Larson's missing toenails, and the whole discussion about moderation and passion. And then my head settled into one thought, the question Kajsa had put to me: *But you must be passionate about something, right?*

What *was* I passionate about? I liked money, but it wasn't a passion. It was hard to be passionate about something you'd never lived without. It was like saying I was passionate about air or water. Though maybe water wasn't the best example, because over the last few days, I'd *almost* become passionate about it.

I certainly wasn't passionate about school or a career. It was practically a joke to suggest it. I didn't have a passionate commitment to family or friends. Friends ... did I even have friends? But was that my fault? It wasn't my idea to ship me around the world and plop me down with strangers. Although I guess it *was* my fault that I had to keep moving.

And it wasn't like I was madly in love with some girl. Or had ever been madly in love. Sure, I'd been out on dates, and I liked girls, but I'd never found anybody who I felt anything special for. The girls I met always seemed so empty, so vacuous—fun to go out drinking with, but maybe a little too much like me. There were a couple of times when I thought something could develop, but then it didn't. It just didn't, because really, what was the point? You get involved, you start to care, and then something happens and it ends.

So I had no answer to the question. It wasn't that I was without passion because I was so moderate. I was no stranger to extreme trouble, and on many occasions I'd been excessively disrespectful, and I'd made it my specialty to drink massive quantities of alcohol … Was that my passion? Was I passionate about drinking?

None of this was helping me sleep. And to make matters worse, the ground underneath me was developing an even bigger tilt—had the stakes on my side been completely exposed? I started to shift farther away, toward the divide between Connor's side and my side, but that was only buying a little more time. Instead I shifted my weight in the other direction until I settled into the ditch the storm had made. I pressed against the outside wall of the tent and wiggled my body into the hole, and right away I felt the warmth of the sand coming through the fabric. The tent wall became taut and the frantic flapping ceased.

Not bad—it was like lying safely in a cocoon. And maybe tomorrow, I'd even come out of that cocoon a different person—a person with passions? No, that was delusional thinking. If I hadn't known better, I'd have thought I was drunk.

CHAPTER FOURTEEN

MY EYES POPPED OPEN. There was light glowing in through the tent walls and there was silence—and then Connor let out a loud snore. The storm was over, the sun was up and we'd both survived.

I sat up, and sand rolled off my sleeping bag. It was coated with sand—everything was coated with sand. I brushed off my arms and my face, and then coughed as I tried to clear my lungs.

I unzipped the sleeping bag and on all fours crawled out of the tent. It sagged badly because the stakes had come free and the roof and sides were weighed down by the sand that had accumulated all night. The second tent looked the same. And where was Larson? He was nowhere to be seen.

It was still so early that the sun was just starting to appear over the big dune to the east and I was in the shade it cast.

"Quite the storm."

I spun around in time to see Larson lying on the ground—or at least Larson's face, the only part of him not buried in the sand! He sat up and the sand spilled off, revealing his sleeping bag. He unzipped it, climbed out and stretched like a big cat. He shook his head and sand rained down from his hair.

"At least this one didn't last long," he said.

"That wasn't long?"

"I was once in a storm that went on for forty-three days."

"Forty-three days!"

"Sometimes it was less powerful and sometimes much more powerful than this one, but it was a constant blow." He shook his head again. "Miserable way to travel, and if the storm hadn't broken, you would have found that out."

"We would have walked in it?"

"Not much choice. We only have enough water for a day or so. We have to get to the next oasis."

"I understand the need to get to an oasis," I said. Thoughts of cool water bubbled in my brain. "But how do you travel if you can't see more than a few feet ahead?"

"You use a rope, and everyone holds on so you stay together."

"But even if we stayed together, wouldn't that just mean we'd be lost together? How would you know where you were leading us?"

"It's hard without the stars or sun to guide me, but I'd follow the compass and just hope for the best."

"And if the best didn't happen?"

"We'd be in the desert without water," he said.

"How far is that oasis from here?" I asked.

"No more than thirty kilometres."

"And we did more than that yesterday, right?"

"Around forty kilometres," he replied.

"So today is shorter ... easier ... right?"

"Shorter, definitely. Easier, we'll see. How are your feet?" he asked.

"I wasn't even thinking of them," I lied. I guess that was really only a *partial* lie, though. As long as I wasn't standing or walking, they didn't hurt. My first few steps of the day had let me know they were going to be a problem. But I didn't want anyone else to know that.

"Well, I hope they're okay," he said, "because as soon as the others are up and everyone's had breakfast, we'll get started again."

I COLLAPSED INTO A HEAP on the sand. All I wanted was to stop. No, that wasn't right. All I wanted was to die and be buried. Buried would have been nice—cool and dark.

Andy, Connor and Kajsa put down their packs. The two guys started to pull out the two tents. Very efficient. I could have helped if I'd been able to get up.

"Are you all right?" Kajsa asked. She looked genuinely concerned.

I wanted to say something flippant and sarcastic. Instead I just shook my head.

"Is it your feet?" she asked.

"My feet and everything they're attached to. Could somebody just shoot me and put me out of my misery?"

"I'm afraid I don't have a gun … here," Andy said. "But it makes you think that all that training we did might have had a purpose after all."

My mind, exhausted and baked, sputtered trying to come up with some brilliant answer. I had nothing, but really there was no point in arguing what was so painfully obvious for all to see. I wasn't prepared.

"But you did really well today," Kajsa said.

"She's right," Connor agreed. "You stayed with us all day."

"How far did we go?"

"Just under forty kilometres," Larson replied.

"That's good … right?"

"That's very good. If we can keep up this pace, we'll reach Tunis on schedule."

Keep up the pace … that was … that was … impossible.

"How long before the sun sets?" I asked.

"Thirty minutes … thirty-five at most."

"I need dark," I said.

"Before it gets dark, I should have a look at your feet," Larson said. "Take off your shoes."

I nodded my head. Slowly, painfully, I removed my shoes and started to peel off my socks.

"Oh, my goodness," Kajsa gasped.

I hardly needed to look because I knew how bad they felt. Still, I looked down, and even I was shocked. My feet were red and puffy and runny and looked like raw meat.

"Kajsa, can you please get me the first-aid kit from my pack? Connor and Andy, please sent up the tents," Larson commanded.

All three instantly set off.

"And boys," he called out after them, "I want you to set the tents up close to the top of the hill ... not the very top but not down here."

I understood the first-aid kit, but why the sudden need for the tents and the specificity of where he wanted them set up? If there was another sandstorm, wouldn't we be better off down low?

A couple of flies settled onto my right foot and I shooed them away. They landed on my left foot and were joined by another fly. I reached down and brushed them away again, but they didn't go far, circling around in the air.

"Flies," I said absently. "Where do they even come from out here?"

"There's lots of life in the desert, but most of it is hidden underground waiting for dark or the right conditions."

"And my feet are the right conditions?"

"The smell of open wounds is what attracted them."

Larson sat down right in front of me and took one of my feet in his hands, examining it. I was just grateful it kept the flies away.

Kajsa walked over and handed him the first-aid kit, then joined the guys in setting up the tents.

"It's amazing what's hidden beneath the surface," Larson said, shooing more flies away from my feet.

"I'm more worried about what won't stay beneath the surface of my skin."

"I was thinking about the desert. Do you know what's beneath us?"

"Sand."

"There's more than that," he said.

"Sand and rock?"

"More."

"Sand and rock and *gravel*?"

He laughed. "Good to see you haven't lost your sense of humour."

"Nope. All I've lost is most of the skin on both of my feet."

"I'll take care of it … as best I can."

The first part of that sentence was reassuring … the second part disturbing.

"How bad is it?" I asked.

"I've seen far worse. Now back to my original

question. Underneath this sand, underneath this rock, is water. Clean, fresh, pure water."

I shrugged. "I guess that makes sense. Since we have the beach already, we might as well have the water to go with it."

He took a knife and started to perform surgery on my feet. "How about if you lie back? It'll be easier for me to work."

I did what he asked, and he kept talking about the water. I think we'd created a quiet conspiracy: he wouldn't tell me what he was doing as long as I didn't ask or look.

"The Sahara wasn't always a desert. If you go back thousands of years, this area received much more rainfall."

"I'd love for it to rain," I said.

"Be careful what you wish for."

"If I was making a wish, it would be for a whole lot of other things."

"I can understand that. Anyway, that rain seeped into the earth into pockets, like underground lakes and rivers and ponds. They call them aquifers. Beneath us is lots of water."

"How far beneath us?"

"It could be less than a hundred feet," he said, "but more likely it's hundreds of feet, perhaps a thousand feet."

"Get me a shovel and I'll start digging," I offered.

He laughed again. "Actually, did you know that *sahara* is the Arabic word for desert?"

"So when we call it the Sahara Desert, we're saying it's the *Desert* Desert?"

"Exactly. Many tribal groups call it *Sahara al-kubra,* which in Arabic means the 'greatest desert.' Which it truly is. It's the largest hot desert in the world."

"As opposed to all the cold deserts?" I joked.

"Well … yes. Strictly speaking, a desert is defined by lack of precipitation, so technically the largest desert in the world is Antarctica. It's fifty percent bigger than the Sahara."

"But doesn't it snow there all the time?"

"It blows there all the time because it's the windiest place on earth, but it hardly ever snows. There are places, the dry valleys, where scientists believe there hasn't been precipitation for thousands of years."

"So this is practically paradise compared to there."

"It is. I was never so cold in my whole life," he said.

"That's right, you've been there … when you climbed that mountain."

"Vinson Massif. And believe me, being in the Antarctic once was bad enough, but the second time was even worse."

"You climbed that mountain *twice*?"

He laughed. "Of course not. The second time I went on snowshoes to the South Pole."

I sat up. "You did what?"

"I walked to the South Pole."

"That's … that's …" I was at a loss for words.

"Cold, really cold."

"That wasn't the word I was going for." I figured it was best not to give him any of the words that were going around in my mind—idiotic, stupid, insane—since he had that knife close by.

"Why?" I asked. "Why did you do that?"

"It's hard to put into words. I guess for the same reasons we're crossing the desert now."

"My father forced you to go to the South Pole to try to teach you a lesson?"

"Okay, not all of us have the same reasons. I guess I just wanted to prove I could do it," he said.

"Prove it to who?"

"Maybe to everybody, including myself. I was younger. Now I don't have anything to prove to anybody."

"So I guess that means you're *not* going to the North Pole next?" I joked.

"No, I do plan to get there someday."

"But if you have nothing to prove … then why?"

"I just always thought it would be cool to stand at the top of the world. Maybe you want to join me?"

I burst out laughing.

"Do I understand that to be a no, or are you so overjoyed at the prospect that you broke into spontaneous laughter?"

"You can take it any way you want. But just for the record, I think you're completely crazy."

"There have been times when I've questioned my own sanity, but I haven't done anything you couldn't accomplish yourself."

"That's even crazier. Just look at my feet after only three days in the desert!" I looked down. They were all bandaged and padded and painted orange with the iodine.

"I've seen worse ... although never this quickly. I think we're going to have to slow down our pace for the next few days. But first things first. We'd all better get into the tents."

"Another sandstorm?" I exclaimed.

"Another storm, but not sand. It's going to rain."

"Come on, quit joking around."

"No joke. Take a deep breath and you can smell it coming."

It was darker now and the wind had picked up. The air was getting cool. I'd thought these were simply signs of night coming. I took a deep breath, and could feel it in my throat and lungs. There was moisture in the air and—

A burst of lightning lit up the sky, followed almost immediately by a clap of thunder!

"We'd better get to the tents," he said.

He offered me a hand up. This time, I took it.

THE LIGHTNING CRACKLED and lit up the whole night sky, and in that light, I saw the looks of amazement, disbelief and fear in the faces of the others. Those were exactly the emotions that rotated through my mind and across my face. All five of us were huddled together in one of the tents. The thunder overwhelmed everything, including the sound of the rain pounding down on the tent.

"I've never seen anything like this," Connor said.

"I don't know if there's ever *been* a storm like this," Kajsa added.

For over an hour we'd watched and listened as the lightning and thunder rolled across the sky. It was eerie and ominous and exciting to watch the storm come to life in the distance, then surround us and then finally engulf us. And by the time it reached us, the interval between lightning burst and deafening thunder was almost non-existent. Then the rain came down. It was as if the heavens had simply opened up and flooded down on top of us.

"It is beautiful, though," Kajsa said.

"It would be more beautiful if we were sitting safely inside a house," I suggested.

"Lightning strikes houses," Andy said. "It generally takes the quickest route to the ground, so it seeks out high objects and metal."

I tapped my finger against one of the metal tent poles.

"We're not going to get hit by lightning," he said.

"We could," Larson said. "Although the risk is very small."

"How small? How much danger are we in?" I asked.

"There are lots of strikes, but it's a very big desert," Larson offered. "The odds are incredibly tiny mathematically."

"Couldn't we have made them smaller if you'd had the guys set up the tents lower down instead of almost at the top of the rocks?" I asked.

"The greater danger is down there. Flooding."

"Flooding … in the desert?" I questioned.

"Obviously you're not a big believer in Noah and his ark," Larson said.

"I'll start to worry when we get halfway to forty days and forty nights of rain."

"That's not going to happen," Larson said. "In fact, I'm sure it's slowing down already."

I listened to the sound of the rain against the tent. It had become much quieter, and I'd already noted in my head that the time between bursts of lightning and the accompanying thunder had lengthened.

"Can we get out of the tent now?" Andy asked.

"Sure, that would be all right," Larson answered.

The zippers on both sides sang out and everybody climbed outside. I clambered out as well, gingerly putting weight on my feet. They were sore, but rest and the treatment had done wonders to make them feel, if not completely better, at least tolerable.

The air was thick and cool and damp, but it was hardly raining at all; it was more of a mist. I closed my eyes and took a deep breath. It was like drinking in the air. It felt so good, all the way down from my mouth and nose to my windpipe and into my lungs.

"I can hear water," Andy said.

Almost instantly headlamps were turned on and aimed in every direction. I turned mine on, too. The beams danced around and—there it was! Down below, running in the bottom of the gully between the dunes and hills, was a stream! Water was racing along in ripples and waves with little whitecaps where it rushed over rocks and bumps.

"Can we get closer?" Connor asked.

"I think we should get close enough to fill our water containers." Larson paused. "All of us except Ethan. You need to get back inside, get your weight off your feet, keep them dry and get to sleep. Any objections?"

I shook my head. "No argument from me."

"Good. I'll check on your feet in the morning before we start walking. Have a good sleep."

CHAPTER FIFTEEN

IF SOMEONE HAD TOLD ME when I woke up the next morning that the whole rainstorm had been nothing more than a mirage or a hallucination or a dream, I'd have believed it. Before we even started to walk, the water had all disappeared. If you looked more closely, you could sort of see patterns in the sand from where it had flowed, but those could just as easily have been caused by the wind. And then, as if it was angry that its work was being imitated, the wind blew sand around to cover up the traces that remained. The only tangible proof of the downpour sat in my water bottle.

Our pace was a little slower that day. I was pretty sure Larson was doing that for my benefit—and my detriment. After all, a longer trip meant less money, but realistically, I knew I wouldn't be able to keep going if we didn't slow down.

Despite the slower pace, I was taking more steps. I'd deliberately shortened my stride to take the pressure off the places that had blisters. That wasn't so easy, because it felt like every spot on both feet was blistered, but the toes and a couple of spots on the pads were the worst. Now if only I could find a way to walk on the tops of my feet, I'd be all set.

Up ahead, Kajsa moved off the path—again—heading for another washroom break. She looked back and gave me an embarrassed smile and a little wave. Not that I was deliberately counting (it was hard to overlook), but this was detour number four, and it wasn't even noon. I was beginning to think she really *did* need to see a specialist.

What I *was* counting was footsteps. I was up to almost eleven thousand. With my normal stride that would have meant eleven kilometres, but I was definitely covering less distance with each step.

Ironically, counting my steps made me forget about the walking. As I'd felt before, there was something about it that was calming, almost like a meditation. In some ways it stopped me from thinking at all. I'd never realized just how many things in my life I didn't want to think about.

I looked up. Connor had stopped to wait, but Andy had kept on going. That surprised me. They always stopped as a group, although I had the sense it wasn't something Andy *wanted* to do. He was like a racehorse—no, a *mechanical* racehorse—and all he wanted was to keep going. It was nothing he'd said so much as his usual expression, a barely noticeable tapping of his foot, a longing look forward, a subtle glance at his watch. It was as though he was counting the seconds. But this time he wasn't counting, he was walking.

I'd stayed close to them all day. Kajsa's washroom breaks had helped make up for my feet. I felt each step, particularly each step with my right foot. Despite my counting, my arithmetic meditation, those were the blisters that hurt the most.

I quickly caught up to Connor.

"How come the Terminator is still walking?" I asked.

"The Terminator?"

"You know, from the movie. *I'll be back*," I said, giving him my best Arnold Schwarzenegger impression. "Doesn't Andy remind you of Arnold?"

Connor laughed. "Maybe a little. Neither one of them wastes many words."

"And both of them might kill you. So why did he keep walking, does he have a date in the future?"

Connor laughed again, and lifted up an arm to offer me a high-five—I guess a congratulation for keeping up with them. For a second I almost didn't respond, but that would have been just plain mean. He'd done nothing to me to warrant meanness. In fact it would have been like kicking a puppy. We exchanged the high-five.

"Way to keep up, buddy!" he said.

As I did every time, I kept walking.

"Keep moving and we'll catch up," Connor called out encouragingly.

This guy was relentlessly friendly. Given another time and place, I think we could have been friends, or at least pretended to be friends.

Andy was well ahead. I couldn't be certain but it seemed he'd opened up a bigger gap between us, that he was walking faster, as if, shed of the weight of his partners, he was able to go quicker. I started digging deeper, walking a little faster myself. For whatever reason, I now felt as though I was in an unofficial race with the Terminator. Better for it to be unofficial. If he knew we were in a race, there was no way he'd let me win.

With each step I felt a little pulse of pain. Okay, maybe pain wasn't the right word, but severe discomfort for sure. None of those burst blisters had become calluses yet, and I could feel where more were forming. Changing my stride to try to avoid putting pressure on the existing sore spots was only creating more sore spots.

Despite my increase in speed, the gap between us continued to grow. Did Andy know we were in a race … or was he just racing everybody? Was he trying to pull ahead and stay in front of the whole "team"? Only one way to find out.

"Andy!" I called out.

He didn't turn around. Either he didn't hear me or

he was ignoring me. But I wasn't somebody who was used to being ignored and I certainly didn't appreciate it.

"Andy!" I yelled, definitely loud enough for him to hear.

He spun around but kept moving, walking backwards!

"Wait up!" I shouted. I started jogging, very slowly. My legs were sluggish and didn't want to move any quicker, and my toes cried out in pain.

He kept walking—backwards. What a bizarre statement. He was waiting up for me, but he *wasn't* waiting for me.

I could see he had his usual serious, stern expression. It was as if there were only so many smiles allowed each day and Connor and Kajsa were using up the whole quota.

As soon as I caught up to him, he spun around and started walking forward again. I had to scramble to match his stride. I could tell within a dozen steps that this wasn't the pace we'd been moving before. He *was* moving faster.

"You're not waiting anymore," I said.

"My knees. If I stop moving, my knees lock up when I start again."

"Maybe the secret is not to start again," I said, and laughed. He didn't laugh. Didn't the Terminator have a sense of humour?

"So you have bad knees," I said.

"Affirmative."

Moving at this speed, I understood the need for one-word answers. It was hard to have the breath for both talking and walking. The best way to slow him down was to get him talking, or at least thinking.

"Bad knees, that's a drag. I guess we all have our own personal odometers."

He gave me a questioning look.

"You know how a car has an odometer that shows how far it's been driving? You figure a car can go maybe two or three hundred thousand kilometres before it's driven into the ground. People are the same way. We only have so many steps in us before we get worn out."

"Not the best analogy. Each person is an individual."

"Just like each type of car is different. You expect to get more kilometres out of a Mercedes than you do a Ford."

"Not necessarily. It depends on how each car is maintained and serviced."

"Definitely, but also how they're driven. A car that's driven hard will break down faster. Just like a person who drives himself too hard can break down his body parts," I suggested.

"That can be mitigated by proper diet and exercise and staying in shape."

"Diet is just giving the engine better fuel, and exercise and staying in shape might just cause the person to break down more quickly," I said.

"That's ridiculous," he snapped.

His response was a bit more emotional than I'd expected. That meant I was zeroing in on something. Had I found the Terminator's weak spot?

"Think about it. Training for a marathon builds up your lung capacity and makes it possible for you to complete the run."

"That's what training is about," he said.

"Yet each step of training takes its toll. Knees and hips are only good for so long, then they have to be replaced … but you'd know about that, wanting to be a doctor and all. Don't old people often need to have hip or knee replacements?"

"Often."

"And I read something about how long-distance runners need joint replacements earlier because of the mileage they rack up and all the pounding they do," I said.

Okay, I hadn't really read that, but it certainly *sounded* plausible. A believable lie was much better than a truth that sounded far-fetched.

"You must have done lots and lots of training for this, and for the other things you've done. I bet *you* put a lot of pounding on your knees," I added.

He didn't answer. I wasn't expecting an answer. It

didn't matter what he said, I just wanted him to listen. I gave it a moment to sink in—which gave me a chance to catch my breath a bit.

"That article detailed a number of endurance athletes who'd had to have their knees replaced by their early forties." I paused. "But I'm sure you'll be fine. You probably won't need to have joint replacement for a long time ... maybe never."

I couldn't be positive, but I thought his footfalls were getting a little lighter, his stride a little shorter.

"Of course, the article said that the majority of endurance athletes *never* need to have anything replaced."

"That's reassuring," he said.

"Yeah, most of them just end up with arthritis. But I'm sure by the time that would affect you, they'll have developed some medication or treatment to control it, so I wouldn't worry."

This time I definitely detected both a change in pace and a slight flicker of reaction in his expression. *Hasta la vista,* baby. I guess I'd sort of terminated the Terminator.

I had him thinking. Now I needed to get him talking. The question was how, but that was kind of a no-brainer. The things people most like to talk about are themselves and their accomplishments, and this guy had some accomplishments to brag about.

"Did you do a lot of training prior to this trip?"

He nodded his head.

Great, a wordless response. Maybe he was thinking so hard about his impending knee surgery that he didn't want to talk.

I tried again. "You ran the Boston Marathon. That must have been exciting."

"Very."

A one-word, two-syllable answer. Not much better. What else had he done? ... Then I remembered.

"I can't believe you rode a bike across the country," I said.

"From sea to sea ... but riding a bike isn't hard on the knees."

"I'm sure it isn't," I said. Thinking *and* talking—this was moving in the right direction. "Can you tell me about it?"

"Do you really want to hear?"

"Of course I do. I'm sure it was really interesting!"

It was probably about as interesting as walking across the desert, which wasn't interesting at all, but it sounded like something *he* found interesting.

"What do you want to know?" he asked.

"Just tell me about it."

He shrugged. "It was last summer. We went west to east, Pacific to Atlantic, so that the prevailing winds would be behind us," he began. "The back wheel of the bike was in the Pacific to begin and then the front wheel was dipped into the Atlantic when we ended."

"How many miles is it in between?"

"Four thousand three hundred and twenty-seven miles is how far we travelled."

I wasn't surprised by him giving the exact distance. I would have been surprised if he hadn't.

"And how long were you on the road?"

"The whole trip took forty-eight days."

Again, very precise—very Andy. "So just under seven weeks."

"We had originally scheduled it to take forty-nine days, so we came in ahead of our ETA," he said proudly.

"You keep saying 'we.' Was it like this trip, with a guide and other people?" I asked.

"No team, no guide. Just me and my dad."

"You spent seven weeks with your father?" That really did surprise me.

"Just the two of us on our bikes."

"That must have been ... been ..."

"Amazing," he said.

That wasn't the word I was struggling to find. I was thinking *painful, annoying, awful*—which is what it would have been like to spend that much time with *my* father. Had we ever spent even seven *days* together? Really, I was trying hard to remember a time when we might have spent seven *hours* alone together.

"We rode side by side and slept in the same tent. Just me and my dad. It was sort of a present for both us before I went off to college."

"And are the two of you still talking?" I joked.

He chuckled. "Of course we are. We've always been close, and that made us even closer. Aren't you close to your father?"

"Pretty close," I lied. On a cosmic scale, if a few thousand miles were close, then we were close. Emotionally we were even farther apart than that.

"It's just … he's pretty busy. There's no way he could *ever* take seven weeks away from work. He's really busy," I said defensively.

"Same with my dad."

"I doubt it's the same," I scoffed. "My father is the CEO of one of the biggest companies in the entire *world*!"

"I guess you're right. The company my father owns only has a few hundred employees. They build locomotives."

"Like, trains?"

"Yeah, trains. He's pretty busy too, but for seven weeks he left the business alone. Not a phone call, not an e-mail and not a text message about business during our whole trip. He said it was my time, and the company would just have to get by without him."

I couldn't remember a single meal with my father that hadn't been interrupted by something to do with business, and it had only gotten worse over the last few years. I wasn't sure he could live without his BlackBerry, and I was pretty sure the company couldn't live without him.

"How did things keep going without your dad there?" I asked.

"He has good people working under him. He just trusted them to make the right decisions."

I couldn't think of one person my father trusted like that. Certainly there was nobody he trusted enough to allow them to run the business. And yet he was prepared to send me around the world to be raised and educated by people he hadn't even met. I guess that said something about which was more important to him.

"Before I left, my father was talking to me about doing it again," Andy said.

"Riding across the country?"

"No, we've been there, done that. We were talking about another adventure. Just me and him, again, spending time together."

"Your father ... you're really close to him, aren't you?" I said.

"He's my dad," he replied simply. As if that was all that needed to be said on the subject.

I slowed down. I didn't want to continue this conversation. Andy slowed down to match my pace. Again a surprise.

"You don't have to wait for me," I said.

"That's okay. We're all going to be stopping soon."

I looked up. On the horizon, like a mirage, was the oasis that was our midday destination.

CHAPTER SIXTEEN

THE WATER BUBBLED UP to the surface and pooled in a large cement trough. From there it leaked out along little plastic tubes that extended and then disappeared under the ground, which was covered with bushes and bulrushes and trees—palm and date and orange. The oranges were very, very little. I had the urge to pull out L'Orange to both introduce him to his kinfolk and also let them see what a *real* orange looked like.

The trees weren't tall, but many were big enough to provide the shade that protected us from the blazing noonday sun. Almost straight overhead, it was unbelievably searing, boiling, broiling, baking hot.

Sitting under these trees with my feet in the cool water, listening to the sound of chirping insects and twittering birds, was as close to heaven as I could imagine. That seemed fair, because it felt as if I'd already walked through hell.

Andy was sitting with his back against one of the trees. His eyes were closed and he was gently rubbing his knees. That gave me a feeling of quiet satisfaction. Connor had his feet in the pool of water as well, and Kajsa was off in the bushes adding her own water to the oasis.

"When do you think Larson will get here?" I asked.

"I don't know, but I'd be pretty happy to spend the rest of the day here," Connor said.

"We need him to come back within the next two hours if we're going to meet our goal for the day," Andy said.

That thought had been in my mind, too. I had only so many days to get to Tunis before I started to lose money. Where was he? I was getting a little annoyed with his frequent and unannounced departures. What sort of guide kept abandoning people—especially in the middle of the desert?

"There he is!" Connor yelled.

I spun around in the direction he was pointing. At first I didn't see anything, and then I caught sight of him, or at least his head, in the distance above a dune. The dark-blue turban stood out clearly against the colour of the sand, but there was something about the movement that seemed wrong, or strange. More of him appeared, and then disappeared, and then reappeared. It was like he was jumping up and down—and then the head of a camel appeared!

"He's riding a camel!" Kajsa shouted as she came back from the bushes.

"That is so cool!" Connor said as he got to his feet. "Maybe he'll let us take a ride on it, too!"

"He'd better let us!" I snapped. "We've been walking all this way and he's been riding a camel? That's not fair!"

And then another head popped up above the dune. Another turban-clad figure. And then a third and a fourth … and all around them were camels! There had to be dozens and dozens of camels, and among the camels were even more goats, scrambling among the oversized feet of the larger animals.

Larson had brought a whole lot of friends—or—was it even Larson? He'd talked about there being nomads in this area. Was this a bunch … a herd … a *tribe* of nomads who were bringing their livestock here to get water? Certainly from this distance there was no way to tell.

"What's that sound?" Andy asked.

I cocked my head to the side. There *was* something, like a buzzing sound. It got louder and clearer until there was no question. It was an engine. Not a plane or even a car or truck. It was too high-pitched. It sounded more like a hive of bees rushing toward us.

A small motorcycle burst over the dune, flying through the air before landing in a spray of sand! Then a second and a third cycle landed right behind the first! The three dirt bikes rounded the dune and then shot off, disappearing from view, the droning sound fading as they raced away.

Andy stood up. He looked a little anxious. If the Terminator was nervous, there had to be a reason, and that made *me* anxious. I pulled my feet out of the water and quickly started to put on my socks and shoes. I figured I should be ready to run if necessary. But run where?

More and more camels and goats kept appearing over the dune until a whole herd was moving toward us—toward the oasis—getting bigger and louder and smellier. There was a distinct odour, probably coming from the camels, as they closed in on us—and that's how it felt, like we were being closed in on, surrounded, trapped. Then the motorcycles reappeared, three abreast, and in front of them were more camels, maybe another three or four dozen. They were being herded, driven, by the men on the bikes.

The four of us crowded together, almost instinctively seeking protection. The camels were coming closer and closer, crowding toward us, rushing forward, bumping and jostling each other, driving the goats ahead of them. It was as if they were being panicked by the motorcycles, as if they were stampeding right toward us and—

"We have to get away from the water!" Connor screamed.

Of course! They were going for the water! We moved backwards and I tripped over my own feet. Andy's grip on my arm was the only thing stopping me from falling down into the sand and under the feet of the onrushing camels!

We moved back into the bushes just as the camels moved right into the space we'd been occupying. The whole herd surged forward, pushing past each other to secure a place at the watering trough. It was a strange symphony of sounds and smells and sights that was overwhelming after the quiet, the emptiness that had been everywhere around us.

There were eight men with dark turbans and flowing robes—eight Larson look-alikes. One of them waved at us. Was that Larson? We all waved back. Either way, we needed to be friendly. One of the mounted camels seemed to collapse, first its front legs buckling and then its back legs—and then a second camel did the same, and a third! They hadn't collapsed, they were just letting their riders down.

It was soon obvious that none of these guys was Larson. They were smaller, darker and looked more like locals. These were real nomads. As they moved toward us, they each smiled and extended a hand in greeting.

"Whoever they are, they're friendly," Kajsa said.

"Whoever they are, they're *armed,*" Andy pointed out.

Each man had a rifle strapped to his back. I had a split second of panic and had to fight the urge to run before I realized that there was no place to go and no way to get away from them if they decided to chase us. We had no choice but to believe the smiles and outstretched hands and not the guns.

One of the men said something to us—something I couldn't understand. I didn't even know what language he was speaking. Was it Arabic?

"*As-salamu Alaykum,*" Andy said.

The man excitedly shook Andy's hand and then kissed him, first on one cheek and then the other!

"What did you just say?" I exclaimed.

"'Peace be with you.' It's an Arabic greeting," he said as the second man began pumping his hand and offering a kiss.

"You speak Arabic?"

"Only how to say hello, goodbye and ask for the toilet. Things I thought might be useful."

Each of the men worked his way down the line, shaking our hands and offering kisses. When they came to Kajsa, they nodded their heads respectfully, but offered neither hands nor lips. I'd have preferred that treatment myself.

One of them started to talk excitedly to Andy. He must have thought he spoke Arabic.

"Sorry," Andy offered, holding his hands up in front of him, "but that's all I can say."

"Ask him for the toilet," I suggested.

"I just wish I could ask him about where Larson is."

"Larson?" one of the men asked.

"Yes, Larson, do you know Larson?" Connor asked.

They all started to talk excitedly, quickly. The only word I could understand was *Larson* and they repeated it continually. Then one of them turned and yelled it out to the others. They all obviously knew him. I just hoped they knew him *and* liked him. He struck me as the sort of guy who you either really liked or really, really didn't like.

The men in front of us now all wore serious expressions. One of them, staring right at me, barked out something that I obviously couldn't understand. The whole atmosphere had changed, and it hadn't changed for the better. If only I could talk to them, I could explain that I wasn't that crazy about the guy either. Strangest of all, even the camels seemed to have changed. Those closest to us were backing away, bumping into others, pawing at the ground.

The man pointed a finger at me and gestured with his other hand for me to be silent. Everyone was serious. No more smiles. But why?

He spoke to me, looking straight at me. At least now his words were soft and calm, though still completely impossible to understand. What was he trying to say to me? I went to take a step forward, and he yelled out something and I froze in place.

Slowly he brushed back his robe and there was a glint of light—sun reflecting off metal. He had a sword strapped to his side. Why would he have a sword, and why was he showing it to me? And then all in one motion, he drew the weapon, raised it above his head and swung it toward me!

And when my life flashed in front of my eyes, it was a very sorry sight.

CHAPTER SEVENTEEN

THE SWORD CUT THROUGH THE AIR, brushing by my side as Kajsa screamed and I jumped, practically knocking over Andy and Connor. In a tangle of arms and legs we scrambled away, my head spinning, trying desperately to think what to do, how to react, where to run and—

"It's a snake!" Kajsa called out.

I looked where she was pointing. The man with the sword was now also holding a snake—no, *two* snakes—no, *one* snake cut into *two* pieces! All the men began smiling again and cheering and patting him on the back. He hadn't been trying to kill me. He'd used the sword to kill a snake that must have been just beside me.

"That's a sand viper," Andy said. "If it had bitten you, you would have been dead within a few hours."

My whole body convulsed.

The man with the sword walked toward me and proudly held up the snake pieces for me to see. "*Voilà!*" he exclaimed.

I backed a step away. Dead or alive, this wasn't something I wanted to handle. Wait, he had said *voilà*. Did he speak French?

"Merci beaucoup," I tentatively said.

His face brightened. *"Parlez-vous français?"*

"Um, *un* little, *petite*, *parle français*."

He started to talk to me in French. Unfortunately my French was only slightly more extensive than Andy's Arabic.

And then Kajsa started talking to him. Obviously she *did* speak French—although as she continued to talk, it was equally obvious that she didn't speak that much French or with much of an accent. I'd been in a couple of international schools in France and travelled enough around the country to at least know what a French accent was supposed to sound like.

She and the men—three of them had now joined the conversation—kept talking. I could tell there was a big communication gap, but I also heard her mention Larson's name again. It was greeted by big smiles and I recognized a couple of words, including *mon ami*. He was a friend—that was very good.

One of them gestured, and at first I thought they were pointing to him, but then I realized they were just aimlessly motioning toward the whole oasis.

Kajsa turned to us. "They know Larson. He's their friend."

"That's good," I said.

"And it's good you speak French," Connor added.

"It would be better if I had more than grade twelve French. Anyway, they say they haven't seen him but that we shouldn't worry. He comes and goes, they said, I think, like the wind."

"That makes sense. He does move like the wind," Connor agreed.

"But the other part doesn't make as much sense," she said. "Maybe I didn't understand ... I probably didn't understand. They said that this whole oasis *belongs* to Larson."

"Can an oasis belong to somebody?" I asked.

"I don't know. It's probably just that I don't understand. Maybe they meant that he's going to be here, or the last place they met him was right here."

"I guess that makes sense," I said.

"And here's a good part—they also offered to feed us. They want to give us a meal."

"I like that idea," Andy said. "Did they say what they were going to feed us?"

"I don't think they're going to order in pizza," I offered. "But what does it matter? Is there any food you don't eat?"

He looked thoughtful. "I'm not really crazy about haggis."

"Then you're probably in luck, unless these guys are part of a lost nomadic Scottish clan."

"Then please tell them we'd be honoured to share a meal with them!" Andy said.

Kajsa translated and the men erupted in cheering and smiling, with more shaking of hands, slapping of backs and more kisses on the cheeks. I wasn't sure if these guys wanted to feed us or take us out on a date. Either way, though, I was pretty sure I'd get something to eat.

OUT OF THE PACKS on their camels they quickly produced, and erected, an open-sided tent. Along with that, just off to the side, two men had dug a pit in the sand and filled it with pieces of wood and what Andy explained was dried camel dung. Apparently it burned well.

"I see the dining room and the stove, but I don't see the meal," Connor said.

"I'm still hoping for pizza or a burger," Andy commented.

"*A* burger?" Kajsa questioned. "As in *one* burger?"

"I was using the term generically. I would like to have many burgers and at least one pizza for myself."

"More likely you're going to get a falafel or a kebab," Kajsa replied. "I'm pretty sure these guys only eat traditional foods."

"Would you consider goat traditional?" I asked.

"Yes, of course, goat is very ..." She got a worried look.

I pointed over her shoulder. I'd been watching as two of the men waded in among the grazing goats. The goats had skittered away—all except one. The two men—one of them holding a large knife—grabbed the goat by the scruff of the neck and started to walk it away. It struggled and kicked and cried out—it sounded almost human, like a baby.

"I can't watch this," Kajsa said. She leaned over and sank her face into Connor's shoulder.

"Circle of life," Andy said. "Better to be at the top of the food chain." He got to his feet.

"Where are you going?" I asked.

"I've never seen a goat slaughtered and butchered. Could be interesting."

"It could be disgusting!" Kajsa snapped.

"It could be both. Anybody else coming?"

Connor shook his head.

"I think I'll pass as well," I said.

"No problem." He pulled his camera out of his pocket. "I'll take pictures, so if you change your mind ... you know ... something to put up on Facebook."

THE SUN WAS ALMOST DOWN and the air was starting to cool off nicely. It certainly hadn't been our plan to stay at the oasis the rest of the day and overnight, but Larson—who'd reappeared sometime after the goat butchering and before dinner—explained that once we'd accepted their invitation to share a meal, we had no choice but to stay. Part of me was upset about losing time, which meant losing money, but mostly I was just happy. I figured I could have pushed myself to travel the distance we were supposed to do today, but I questioned what state I would have been in the next day or the day after. My feet needed a rest. All of me needed a rest.

It was amazing to me that after being isolated in the desert for only a few days, it felt so strange to be surrounded by living things. Goats and camels wandered about grazing and watering. And of course there were the nomads, gathered around the fire. Below the ashes and embers, the goat was cooking … well, I guess baking, really.

Andy and Connor and Kajsa were now clustered around the fire pit, probably drawn by the wonderful aromatic smell. As for me, I was enjoying being alone. Well, almost alone.

I dug into my pocket and pulled out L'Orange of Tunisia. He was looking a little worse for wear, a bit more shrivelled and pushed in and no longer round.

"Bad day, huh?" I asked L'Orange.

He didn't answer.

"That's okay, I don't like complainers anyway. It's not like anybody is going to want to hear you complain."

I took L'Orange in my hands and tried to form him back into a sphere, with some success.

"There, that must feel better. Now if you could just do something about my feet. Would orange juice help blisters?"

I sensed a movement just to my side. A shudder ran through my whole body when I thought it might be another viper. I almost didn't want to look. Maybe if I didn't see it then it wouldn't be there.

"Sorry to disturb your conversation." It was Larson.

I closed my hand over L'Orange and turned it over so that it wasn't so visible. "Sometimes the most intelligent conversation you can have is with yourself," I joked.

"I don't know if it's the most intelligent, but it might be the most agreeable."

"Lots of people talk to themselves," I said. I'd rather he thought I was talking to myself and not an orange. One was eccentric, but the other was just a little this side of crazy.

"I spend so much time alone in the desert that I talk to myself just so I can hear a human voice," Larson said. He sat down beside me. "It smells good."

"Really good," I admitted.

"It puts us behind schedule, but we couldn't turn down their invitation to share a meal," he said. "Especially after what happened with the snake."

I felt an involuntary shudder go through my whole body. "If that snake had bitten me, would I have died?"

"There's a possibility that you just would have been really sick. It depends on how much venom it injected and your body's reaction. Everybody is different."

"Maybe it wouldn't even have bitten me," I said.

"Maybe."

"But maybe he saved my life. I guess I should be grateful."

"Mohammad was asking me about you."

"Mohammad?" I asked.

"The man who killed the snake," he explained. "Have you heard the saying that if you save somebody's life, you're responsible for them?"

I shook my head. "Never heard of it, and now that I have, I'm not even sure what it means."

"Because Mohammad saved your life, he feels that he has responsibility for it. So, for example, if he saved your life and then you killed somebody, *he* would be the cause of that death."

"You can tell him that I promise not to kill anybody."

"He wanted to know if you were a good person."

I almost didn't want to ask the question, but I had to. "What did you tell him?"

"I told him that you were in the process of becoming an *even better* person."

"And that means?"

"It means that the *you* of a few days ago would have been trying to figure out how to bribe somebody or steal a motorcycle so you could get to Tunis."

I smiled. I'd thought of both, but the language barrier stopped me from doing the first, and the absence of a key to one of the motorcycles or a map to get to Tunis basically eliminated the second.

"I'm trying."

"You're succeeding." Larson got to his feet. "Time to eat."

He offered me his hand, which I took. He pulled me up and we started walking. It worked in my favour, I was thinking, that Larson believed I'd do the right thing. It would make it that much easier to do what I needed to do when the time arrived. It wasn't just that I didn't want to walk to Tunis, it was that I was becoming more doubtful that I could.

I limped over to the fire.

CHAPTER EIGHTEEN

I LEANED BACK AND LOOKED UP, watching the ashes thrown off by the embers drifting up into the sky. It was as if they were flying up to join the stars that were millions of brilliant pinpricks punctuating the night sky. Sitting all around the fire were the five of us and our nomad friends. All were men except Kajsa. I think she was not only aware of it but a little uncomfortable, because she hadn't gone to the bathroom very often. She seemed to be reassured by having either Larson or one of the guys close at hand.

We'd all eaten goat and rice and cornmeal. Our hosts had made a feast for us, and I'd eaten a lot—although I'd kind of avoided the goat. It unnerved me to think I was eating something that had been alive just a few hours before. I'd moved the piece I'd been given around my plate, hiding it among the rice and cornmeal until now there wasn't any food to hide it behind. I knew I couldn't just put my plate down because that might offend them, and I figured it wasn't smart to offend people with swords and rifles.

Looking at the number of pieces that Andy had eaten, I had a pretty good idea of how to get rid of it.

I extended my plate to Andy. "You want another piece?"

"Don't mind if I do," he said. He used a fork to transfer the goat onto his plate. "Thanks."

"I think with this piece, you've eaten almost a whole goat by yourself," Connor said.

"Well, I know it's fresh ... really fresh," he joked.

Larson said something in Arabic and all the men began laughing. He turned to Andy. "I told them that the way you eat, they should have slaughtered a camel instead of a goat."

Andy finished chewing and swallowed down the mouthful. "What does camel taste like?"

"Probably like chicken," Connor said. "Doesn't everything taste like chicken?"

"Not everything," Larson said, "and believe me, I've eaten a whole lot of things that make camel seem like hamburger."

Then Mohammad said something to Larson, who laughed.

"Our host says he'd like to tell you a story ... well, he'll tell me a story and I'll translate it for you."

Mohammad began to talk. I couldn't understand the words, but there was a lot of expression in his voice. His gestures were big, and he seemed to really be into what he was saying. The other nomads sat cross-legged and listened intently. He stopped and motioned for Larson to translate.

"I won't be able to tell the story with the eloquence of Mohammad," he began, "but I'll try. Mohammad asked if you've heard about genies in a bottle."

We all nodded politely. I hated fantasy and fairy tales.

"He said that you need to know that they're not pretend, they're real. He said that as you walk across the desert, you might find one. In fact, he himself found one."

Oh great, the guy with the sword, the guy who'd saved my life, was about to tell us some lame story and I'd have to pretend to be interested.

Larson nodded at Mohammad, who began to talk again. This time he didn't just talk, he got up and started to act out something. He wasn't much of an actor—or I guess a mime, since we didn't understand the words—but he certainly seemed to be enjoying himself. All the men—including Larson—nodded along. They were enjoying his story, too. I figured that when you lived in the desert with no TV, radio, telephones, MP3 players or Internet, this was what qualified as quality entertainment.

Mohammad stopped talking and Larson began again.

"So, Mohammad was walking through the desert,

and he hates to admit it, as both a man and a Berber, but he was lost."

"Nomads get lost?" Connor asked.

"Even nomads. So he was wandering around, lost, disoriented, almost out of water, when he tripped and fell flat on his face. As he turned around, he saw this shiny object that he'd tripped over, and out of it came smoke, and that smoke became a genie, a gigantic genie!"

Now some of the gestures Mohammad had been making made more sense.

"He's not ashamed to say he was afraid, but the genie spoke to him and assured him that not only should he not be afraid but that this was his lucky day, because the genie was going to grant him two wishes."

"Two wishes?" I asked. "I thought it was *three* wishes."

"No, definitely two," Larson said, holding up two fingers. He looked at Mohammad, who also held up two fingers and nodded.

"I think the three wishes is from a Disney movie," Larson said. "This is a *real* story."

Mohammad started talking again. Once more his voice was expressive. He acted out the scene as the men watched him with rapt attention. I just sat there, helpless, waiting for him to end so that Larson could translate and we could get this story over with.

Suddenly, unexpectedly, all the men, including Larson, burst into laughter. Two of them jumped to their feet and slapped Mohammad on the back. I was now at least a little interested in what he'd said.

"Okay, so the genie told Mohammad he had two wishes," Larson said. "And of course his first wish, as you can imagine, was that he be transported to a place where he had food and water and where he wasn't lost. So the genie blinked his eyes, and instantly they were at an oasis—in fact *this* oasis—and all around him were his friends and family, including his wife."

What a coincidence that we were sitting in the exact same place.

"So," Larson continued, "the genie asked him what his second wish was, and Mohammad told him that he'd always wanted to visit New York City, but that he didn't want to fly and he didn't like ships. He wished to travel to New York on his camel. So he asked the genie if he could build a bridge between Africa and America. Well, the genie explained that he was a very powerful genie, but that was just too difficult. He asked Mohammad to make another wish.

"Now, Mohammad was much younger then and had only recently married, and he was finding that he didn't understand what his wife wanted from him sometimes, and because of that, they fought, and Mohammad is a man of peace."

I thought I could tell that by the rifle and the sword.

"So Mohammad asked the genie if he could give him the power to understand women. The genie looked at Mohammad and said, 'Do you want that bridge to be two lanes or four?'"

We all broke out laughing—including me. It wasn't even that the joke was that funny, but it just felt so good to laugh. I tried to stop, but I kept giggling and laughing so hard that tears came to my eyes.

Mohammad stood up and took a bow and we all cheered. He then started to speak. Was he telling another joke?

"Mohammad has now said that he'd like to share one more thing with his guests. With your permission, he and some of his friends would like to play music for you."

"That would be amazing!" Kajsa exclaimed, and Connor and Andy and I all enthusiastically nodded in agreement.

One of the men pulled out a small metal and wood instrument—it looked like a flute, but it wasn't.

"That is the Arabian *ney,*" Larson explained. "And having heard him play, I can tell you that he's a very skilled performer."

He began to play. The music was high-pitched and sharp but incredibly melodic. Mohammad's fingers raced up and down the little instrument and the notes jumped free. It wasn't anything I recognized, but it was good.

Suddenly the sound of the *ney* was joined by a beat. Two of the other men were using water containers like drums. Then another man began to sing along. All three—voice, drums and *ney*—blended together perfectly.

There was such a sense of balance, of order, as if this was exactly what *should* happen. The sound was almost hypnotic. I lay on my back on the sand, the music all around me, staring up at the sky above, and felt at peace, at ease, as if somehow this was where I was supposed to be. It all felt so … so … strange.

I sat bolt upright. This *wasn't* where I belonged. I shouldn't be here. Not with these people, not being forced to do what I was doing. I wasn't going to get sucked into this. I stood up, and without saying a word, I went to my tent.

CHAPTER NINETEEN

THE MUSIC WENT ON for more than an hour. I couldn't really tell for sure because I'd lost track of time and I wasn't going to turn on my headlamp to check. I didn't want them even to know I was still awake. I lay there, thinking, wondering, questioning, part of me longing to go back outside and join in the music and conversation and laughter, but the bigger part of me wanting to stay outside their circle. I wasn't going to be tricked or bribed or coerced or fooled into being a member of this little group. I wasn't part of their "team." I wasn't buying in to their story about being proud of working together and achieving some pointless accomplishment. I was too smart to be a lemming or a sheep. We weren't going to suddenly bond and become lifelong *best friends forever,* and this wasn't going to change my life. Did my father—did Larson—actually think that some little light bulb was going to go off in my head, and that I'd see the errors of my past and be transformed into somebody new, somebody different, somebody they thought was good? That *wasn't* going to happen.

I knew I had to be more careful from now on and not let my defences down, not get sucked in. Nobody gets in, nobody gets any closer. I wouldn't make that mistake again.

The music stopped. Was it a break between pieces or had the night finally come to a merciful end? Voices came closer and I heard footsteps. The beam from a flashlight passed by the tent, and then there was the sound of the zipper opening up. I turned away from Connor's side of the tent, certain that in the darkness I could easily pretend to be asleep. There was nothing I wanted to say and nothing I was going to ask.

Connor climbed into the tent, shaking out his shoes and then closing the zipper behind him to seal out the scorpions, spiders, vipers and at least some of the sand—assuming we didn't have another sandstorm.

He used his headlamp to see so that he could settle in for the night. I could *feel* him moving around, and then, listening closely, I could hear him humming one of the songs from around the campfire. I recognized the tune because I'd been humming it to myself before he got here.

"Ethan, are you awake?"

His question startled me for an instant. Slowly,

sleepily, I turned around. He was sitting on his side of the tent looking through the mesh.

"I'm awake now," I muttered.

"Sorry, I just thought the music would have kept you up."

"It did, for quite a while."

"It was pretty amazing, wasn't it?" he asked, sounding as enthusiastic as ever. This guy was like the Energizer Bunny of happiness.

"I just wanted to thank you again for being the one sharing the tent and putting up with my snoring," he said.

"Maybe you should thank me for putting up with your talking when I'm trying to sleep. How about turning off the light so I can get *back* to sleep?"

He turned off the light and the tent became dark once again.

"Ethan?"

I sighed. "Yes?"

"Thanks also for putting up with my talking."

He giggled and I turned over, stifling the urge to giggle, too.

I knew when Connor had dropped off to sleep because he started snoring. And I'd learned that waking him up would give me only a few minutes of respite before he started snoring again. When he slept, he snored. The only way to keep him from snoring was to keep him from sleeping. But how?

Maybe I could unsettle his thoughts. I mean, I liked the guy, but as I said, we weren't going to be best friends—that just wasn't going to happen. And it was his turn to be on the receiving end of some of my patented mind games. But how did you unsettle somebody who didn't seem to have a care in the world? Then it came to me—he'd already apologized for talking; I'd just take it one step further.

"Connor, wake up!" I called out.

He snorted louder and then woke up. "Um … sorry … was I snoring again?"

"Not snoring, you were talking in your sleep," I said.

"Talking. I didn't know I did that."

"You do. Really loud, but not so clear." I paused.

"What was I talking about?" he asked, sounding both interested and much more awake. He turned on his headlamp, sat up and looked through the mesh at me.

"It was hard to tell … really … it just seemed like you were really upset … like you'd been hurt."

"Like somebody had punched me?" he asked.

"More like somebody had broken your heart." I paused. "She really did hurt you, didn't she?"

"What?"

"The girl. She really hurt you badly."

I was just taking a guess, but I could tell by the look in his eyes that maybe I had hit something. Then again, who hasn't been hurt by somebody at some point?

"I couldn't even make out her name. You were mumbling but you kept saying her name again and again and—"

"Was it Ashley?" he asked.

"That's it, Ashley! I couldn't tell if it was Ashley or Ashton or—"

"Ashton is a guy's name!" he exclaimed.

"I just knew your heart had been broken. I'm not here to judge or—"

"*Her* name is Ashley!"

"Sorry, I didn't mean to imply anything. Look, I don't know you that well ... I know you probably don't want to talk about it, but it's obviously still pretty tender since you're talking about her in your sleep."

He let out a big sigh. "I thought I was over her ... over it."

"Obviously not. You know, denial is not just a river in Egypt."

"What?"

"Bad joke. I was saying that obviously you're not, that you're just denying it. Whether you talk about it or not, it's still here," I said, touching my heart, "and here," touching my head. "No matter how much you think you can push it down, it still bubbles to the top. That's how the subconscious works."

He nodded his head knowingly.

"You know what Freud said."

"I don't even know anybody named Freud."

"Sigmund Freud, you know, the father of modern-day psychoanalysis," I explained. I'd just finished a big assignment on him, so I'd be able to throw out a few quotes and fake enough insights to make it sound as though I knew what I was talking about. I'd gotten a good mark on that assignment ... which made sense, since I'd paid good money for it. It was amazing what you could find on the Internet.

"Oh yeah, sure, of course. So what did he say?"

"He said that the mind is like an iceberg. It floats with only one-seventh of its bulk above the water."

"So a lot of what we think and feel we don't really show, right?" Connor said.

"Not in your conscious mind, but it's all there in your subconscious. Even when you don't talk about it or think about it, it still bubbles up from underneath when you can't defend yourself, like when you're really tired or you've had too much to drink."

"Or when you're sleeping."

"Exactly."

"Sounds like you know a lot about this stuff."

"I'm interested in psychology," I said. That was no lie. I was interested in anything that would help me understand and then be able to manipulate or control other people. Psychology was useful for that, and this was a case in point. I'd certainly gotten into his psyche.

"You really are pretty smart about things," Connor said.

Toss around enough quotes and you look smarter and more insightful than you are. Quote Gandhi and Mother Teresa and you look like a saint.

"Freud also said, and I quote, 'We are never so defenceless against suffering as when we love, never so forlornly unhappy as when we have lost our love object or its love.'"

"Wow, that's so ... so deep."

"He was a pretty smart guy."

"Like you," Connor said.

"And if you don't talk about things, they get stuck inside of you because you're repressing them. It's sort of like if you don't take out the garbage it starts to stink inside."

"Did Freud say that as well?"

"Something like that ... not an exact quote." I was just making things up now. I could probably throw in some song lyrics and he wouldn't know any better.

"You know, talking is good for the soul," I suggested.

"I just couldn't talk to anybody about how I was feeling. I didn't want to worry my parents and I didn't want my friends to think I was so whipped."

"True friends wouldn't judge you," I said.

"I would *really* like to talk about her. There's so much I need to get out. Could I talk to you?"

"You can talk to me," I said, "but not now. Tomorrow. It's the middle of the night and we both need to sleep."

"I don't even know if I *can* sleep."

"Maybe it's even better that you don't," I said.

"Really?"

Now I had to think up a reason for that, other than *so I can sleep*.

"You can spend the rest of the night thinking, letting things come to the surface in your head, and then tomorrow, when we're walking, we'll have plenty of time."

"We will have plenty of time. I just don't want to talk in front of everybody else. It's sort of private, you know, embarrassing."

"No problem. It's a big desert, and we can walk behind or in front of them and talk." Well, he could talk and I could pretend to listen. "But right now I have to go to sleep. Can you turn off the light again, please?"

"Sure, of course."

Once again it got dark and I settled into my sleeping bag. The darkness hid my smug expression. This was easy. Very easy.

"Ethan?" Connor said softly.

This wasn't part of the plan.

"Thanks ... and good night."

"You're welcome ... and good night, too."

I rolled over and away from him. I felt a pang of guilt, and that surprised me. Why should I feel guilty? It wasn't me or anybody else who'd forced him to come on this insane expedition. The only one here against his will, the only one here who'd been abandoned in the desert, was me. But still, I felt guilty.

CHAPTER TWENTY

IT WAS BARELY SUNRISE, but Mohammad, the rest of the nomads, and their camels and goats and motorcycles were all gone. If it hadn't been for their footprints leading away from the oasis, the whole thing could have been a mirage. It was the sound of those motorcycles that had finally jarred me out of semi-sleep.

I'd been awake a good part of the night not listening to Connor snore. He had obviously stayed awake thinking, and I'd stayed awake feeling guilty about making him stay awake. Why was this bothering me so much? I'd just met the guy a few days ago, and it wasn't like he was a friend ... well, not a real friend. Did I even have one of those? And *was* there anybody or anything that made me feel passionate? This was garbage thinking.

I heard the sound of a zipper and turned around in time to see Connor climbing out of the tent.

"Good morning, buddy," he said cheerfully.

Up half the night and still happy. I wasn't sure what

drugs this guy was on, but I definitely wanted to speak to his doctor.

"A good morning would be me waking up in a real bed in a real house in a real city," I said.

"Seriously, is there any place else you'd rather be this morning?"

I laughed. "Weren't you listening? Real house, real city ... any real city, but I'd be willing to start with Tunis."

I walked over to where the fire had been and where Kajsa was already sitting. She really should have been the type of girl I was attracted to—tall and blond and pretty—but she lacked one important element I needed. She was neither damaged nor lacking in confidence. Aside from her little worries about her bladder—worries I'd planted there myself—she was completely self-assured. I hated that in a girl.

She had put out the cookies and was just getting out the bread and marmalade. There were flies buzzing all around the food. The camels and goats seemed to have left behind some of their entourage.

"Hungry?" she asked, offering me a piece of bread.

"Hungry, yes ... for that, probably not."

I reached down and grabbed some cookies. They contained chocolate, sugar and starch—the breakfast triumvirate of carbo-loading before setting out on another wonderful day of walking across the desert.

Involuntarily I moved my toes up and down in my shoes. They were sore but not really painful. A half-day's rest instead of a full day's wear had had a positive effect. I guessed the only question was how long that was going to last. By the end of the day I might not be any better off than I'd been at the end of the day before.

I caught sight of Andy coming out of the dunes. He was moving slowly, and there was something about his expression that didn't seem right. His normal look of determination was undermined by a hint of doubt. What was that about?

"How are the knees?" I asked, trying to sound both innocent and caring.

"A little sore, but it isn't my knees that are the problem ... I gotta run."

He spun around and quickly ran back in the direction he'd just come from, disappearing behind a dune.

"What's wrong with him?" I asked Kajsa.

"I think that goat he ate last night isn't agreeing with him," she said. "He's not doing well at all."

"Really?"

"That's his fifth trip behind the dunes. He looks awful, and when I offered him some food he just ran off, gagging."

"Andy turned down food?" Connor asked as he walked over. "That's serious."

"Maybe he's just making room for more food. He

did eat most of a whole goat by himself last night," I offered.

"I wonder if he's going to be able to walk today," Kajsa said.

That thought hadn't even occurred to me. I couldn't imagine anything stopping Andy, especially not a little roasted goat … okay, a lot of roasted goat. Those Terminator movies would have been far less exciting if all they'd had to do was feed the cyborg some goat meat. *I'll be back … but first I have to use the washroom.*

This was not good. We'd already lost a half-day's travel time.

"Where's Larson?" I asked Kajsa.

"Filling the water containers," she said, pointing to the trough.

I walked over. He seemed so intent on what he was doing that he didn't notice me until I was practically standing over him.

He looked up. "This is one of my favourite places in the world. I think I could stay here forever," he said.

"That's good for you, but it doesn't work for me. I can't afford to waste any more time here."

"Time cannot be wasted or saved or spent, it simply is," he stated.

"And I'd rather be sailing," I said.

He looked confused.

"My other car is a Porsche."

"I don't understand," he said.

"If you can read this, you're too close."

He looked more confused. It was nice that he was the one who was confused for a change.

"I still don't understand what you're saying."

"I'm quoting my favourite bumper stickers," I said. "Isn't that what you were doing when you said that garbage about time not being wasted or saved? I assumed you got that from a bumper sticker. Oh, I forgot, no bumpers around here, so maybe it was on the side of a camel."

He didn't react, not even with a change in expression. Very Zenlike.

"Maybe time can't be saved or spent," I continued, "but money can. If I don't get to Tunis on time, then I lose money, right?"

"That was your father's idea, an incentive to keep you moving."

"Well, I want to get moving, and I couldn't yesterday because of those nomads making a meal for us."

"A very good meal," he said.

"Yeah, tell that to Andy. And speaking of Andy, if he can't walk today because he's too sick, am I going to be penalized for that as well?"

"You are a member of a team."

"Like I've said, I didn't sign up for any of this, including all that crap about us being a team. Just because I'm forced to occupy the same piece of ground with other people doesn't mean that I'm on the same team, or that I even like them."

"If any member of the team couldn't travel, we would all have to wait," he said.

"And like I keep saying, I'm not part of any team. You should do what you promised my father and be my guide and get me there on time!"

"I'm not leaving anybody behind, but if you wish, I could speak to your father and explain it wasn't your fault that you couldn't get there on time."

"You really *don't* know my father at all," I scoffed. "With him, a deal is a deal. He's not going to renegotiate. That's not the way he does business."

"But this isn't about business. This is about something so much more important."

"Wrong again. For my father *nothing* is more important than business!" I didn't need to say *including me,* because I think we already knew that. "So what's it going to be? Are we leaving or aren't we?"

"We're leaving. All of us together, at whatever speed the least of us can manage," he said.

"Great. You might as well stick a gun to my head and rob me that way."

"No one is going to rob you," he said. "I'll give you one more bumper sticker quote. *If you wish to move quickly, go alone. If you—*"

"Are you telling me to go out there by myself?"

"Listen for the whole saying. *If you wish to move quickly, go alone. If you wish to go far, go together*."

"I need to travel quickly *and* far, so what's your response to that?" I demanded.

He didn't answer. I guess he didn't have another bumper sticker saying to throw at me.

CHAPTER TWENTY-ONE

I CAME TO THE CREST of the hill and looked back, waiting for them to appear over the last rise before I descended this one. The terrain was hardscrabble, with scrub plants, lots of rock, hard-baked sand that left only partial tracks, and hills. My visions of a desert being flat had long since been abandoned. There were lots and lots of ups and downs.

It was hard on the legs and lungs to climb, but not that much easier on the legs on the way down. I'd never imagined down being a problem, but it was. The pressure points inside my shoes against my feet made the old blisters painful and created new ones. And my stride was different again today. A different stride led to different blisters.

There was a slight breeze, but like everything in the desert, it was boiling hot. It didn't so much cool as complete the cooking process. And there wasn't a cloud in the entire sky to offer even the hope of shade. Not one puff of white in the whole brilliant blue sky to hide behind.

I looked at my watch. It was just after ten and we'd been walking for a little more than three hours. We hadn't moved fast, but we had kept moving.

"Come on, hurry up," I muttered to myself. Talking to myself was not a good sign.

I rummaged around in my pocket and pulled out two oranges. One was a recent addition—I'd pulled it out of our food supplies just before we left. The other was my good friend L'Orange. In some ways he was my best friend on this trip. At least he wasn't the one making demands on me or holding me back, making me stand here in the hot sun waiting instead of moving forward. L'Orange was a *true* friend.

I guess I *could* have moved forward. It wasn't like we were tied together by rope, and I did know where we were going. Larson had told me that we'd be following behind the nomads and their herds for the first half of our journey today. It was a little unnerving to be out of sight of the others, though. I wasn't going to walk beside them, but it was good to at least see them. On the plus side, I could still see the tracks of my nomadic guides. Maybe the ground was harder now, but there were still tracks. Big clear camel tracks. They were my guides.

Then the rest of them appeared over the rise and I felt a sudden sense of release and relief. One, two, three and then all four came into sight. They were just four little darker dots on the landscape. If I hadn't known who they were, it would have been impossible to identify them from this distance. But I could tell which was which. Connor and Kajsa were slightly in the lead, walking side by side, and Andy and Larson were behind.

They were moving slowly, following in my tracks as I had followed in the tracks of the nomads and their livestock.

Part of me was resentful that I had to keep waiting for them to appear. Another part was quite proud. I *wasn't* proud that I was crossing the desert—that was just stupid—but I was proud that I was showing them up, at least for the day.

For the first couple of hours, before the terrain had changed and before I'd opened up a sizeable lead, I'd watched as they made frequent stops—both for Andy and for Kajsa. But still, I had to give them all my grudging admiration. Andy—who'd looked like he was either dead or at least wanted to be—kept going. I chuckled: *dead man walking*. I had to think that, in some small way, I was even a little bit responsible for him moving at all. I knew it bothered Andy that some no-training screw-up like me was ahead of him, and that had to be what was driving him, making him keep moving forward even when he probably shouldn't have been.

And then there were Kajsa and Connor. They'd taken some of the load from Andy's pack, so he was carrying less weight and they were carrying more. I could have offered to take some as well, but I didn't. I wasn't part of their team, and doing that would have made it seem like I was. Although I thought that maybe, just maybe, I would have helped Connor or even Kajsa.

I figured this looked good on the Terminator. If you eat a whole goat, you'd better expect to have some problems. Revenge of the goat.

They started descending the rise and I decided it was time for me to get moving again. The next stop, after which the nomads were going to take a different route from us, was an abandoned settlement that Larson had described to me. It was still at least two hours away, but I knew that when I got there I'd have a chance to sit in the shade for a while. Who knows, I thought, I might even have a nap while I was waiting for them to follow.

I walked down the hill and they vanished from view. I had a feeling of uncertainty and anxiety as I walked down. It was the same feeling I'd had on the first night when I left them behind at the fire and went over the dune to relieve myself. But I had no reason to be anxious now. I had tracks to follow. It was all good. I'd just keep saying that to myself until I started to believe it.

I slipped L'Orange back into my pocket. I didn't want him to see what was going to happen next with the other orange. It wasn't going to be pretty, but it certainly was going to be tasty.

WITH THE EXCEPTION of the occasional lizard and one big scorpion, I hadn't seen any other life form for almost two hours. It was noon, and the sun was at its highest point. We were supposed to be at the ruins before this, but here I was still walking, still in the sun, still not sitting down in the shade. All this waiting for Kajsa and Andy, a few minutes here and a few minutes there, had eaten into our time and put us behind schedule. Finally I'd made a decision not to wait any longer. I needed shade and rest and water more than I needed to see them behind me. Besides, it didn't matter what was behind me as long as I had what was in front of me—the trail leading me forward.

Over the past thirty minutes, as the distance had grown between me and the others, the trail had been easier to follow. It wasn't even a challenge to pick up the tracks anymore. I figured it had to do with the ground becoming more sandy and soft, and gaining ground on the nomads and their herds. Again, not a source of pride, but definitely an accomplishment.

I put my head down and started walking again. I didn't care about my feet hurting or my legs being sore. The only way to relieve either was to keep taking steps, one after the other, until I got to a place where I didn't have to move anymore for a long time. I felt the slight rise of the hill in my legs and lungs, but I wasn't going to listen to what they were telling me. A few more steps and I'd get to the top of another hill. And then, unbelievably, there were camels on the other side! I hadn't just gained ground, I'd caught up with them!

I looked around for Mohammad or any of the others ... or goats ... or motorcycles ... I guess these were just some of their camels, but where were *they*? And then I had another thought, one I almost couldn't allow myself to think about. These camels weren't part of the nomads' herd. These were wild camels, and I was following their tracks—tracks that had led me into the middle of the desert ... the middle of nowhere ... by myself ... alone.

As I stood there, trying to think, the camels moved off, disappearing behind an outcrop of rock and sand. I had to fight the urge to run after them so that at least I wouldn't be alone. But the part of me that was still trying to make sense of everything knew that was just plain insane. And I was reassured to know that I wasn't fully insane ... yet. I told myself to think it through. I was here because I'd followed their tracks. If I'd followed them in one direction to get lost, I could just as easily follow them back in the other direction to get found. Okay, it was going to take a lot more time, and it meant that I'd be walking in the wrong direction, but there was nothing I could do about it and certainly no need to panic. Well, at least not yet. There'd be plenty of time for that later.

CHAPTER TWENTY-TWO

I PULLED OUT the last two things in my pack—the sleeping bag and the headlamp. Everything else, item by item, had been discarded over the passing hours. I couldn't even imagine how far I'd travelled, first following the tracks of that herd of camels, and then finding more tracks and more tracks, and then, once the wind kicked up, not having any tracks to follow whatsoever.

The sun was starting to set. I was both relieved and terrified: grateful for the shadows I could hide in and afraid of what the night would bring. The only reason I'd kept the two items I had was the night. I needed that headlamp; to be in the dark alone would have been suffocating. And the sleeping bag would be my only protection from the cold and elements. The desert was nothing but extremes—way too hot during the day and way too cold at night. I had thoughts of wrapping myself in the nylon and going to sleep, and either waking up someplace else ... or simply not waking up. Had it come to that already, that I was thinking about dying?

I'd been rationing my water as best I could, trying not to drink more than half a litre each hour. I'd had three litres when I got lost, and that was almost six hours ago. I tipped back the bottle and the last few drops trickled into my mouth. That was it. That was it for all my water. I dropped the bottle into the sand.

As I stood there I watched as my tracks, hardly a minute old, were erased, filled in by the wind and the sand. The wind had continued to pick up, obliterating any sign of where I'd been and where I should go. I wondered how long it would be until the sand covered *me* up, until there was no trace of me ever being here. Then I tried to figure out how long they'd search until they realized there was no point in searching any longer. And who could blame them for stopping? What was the point in risking lives to find a body ... especially my body? Who really cared? It wasn't like I'd done anything that would make them want to try to find me. They were probably all sitting around a fire, eating, having a good laugh, glad to be done with me.

No, that wasn't who they were. Certainly not Connor or Kajsa. Certainly not Larson, who respected all life, and not Andy. Maybe he was the Terminator, but he would willingly go back in time to save lives—even a life as worthless as mine.

There was a rise up ahead. Against my will and against gravity, I'd force myself to climb it. It was harder with each hill because I was no longer able to use the buoyancy of hope to help me climb, believing, the way I had the first fifty times, that once I'd crested the hill I'd see them. But still, there was the tiniest little glimmer of hope, and that was all that kept me moving.

Where there's life, there's hope. I chuckled to myself. My brain was so fried that I was talking in bumper sticker sayings. Larson would be so proud of me. Shame my father wouldn't be. My death would be just one more screw-up, one more way that I'd failed to live up to expectations. I'd die the way I lived, a failure.

The hill was taller than the others I'd climbed. Or maybe it just seemed higher. It was steep and made of rock and sand. As I got close to the top I realized I was going to have to leave the shelter of the shade. I stopped climbing. I didn't want to go back out into that sun. It was like it was an animal, a dangerous animal that I needed to avoid, needed to escape. Here I was safe, out of its grip, away from its fangs and claws.

Anyway, what was the point in going on? When I got to the top, I'd see there was nothing, nobody, and that last little flicker of hope would be snuffed out—because I knew this was the last hill I was going to climb today ... maybe the last hill I was going to climb ever.

At least down at the bottom I could live with the belief that they were just on the other side. I could lay down my head and rest, let the darkness surround me, go to sleep, dream, pretend ... deny. Better just to give up and give in, because whether I climbed the hill or not, I was going to die.

Going to die ... now that was a bumper sticker for you. We were all going to die. I just hadn't figured my death would be so soon, and so strange, and so pointless. Pointless, like my life.

I was going to die. That thought should have terrified me. Instead it was almost a relief. It was as though a weight had been lifted off my shoulders. I took a deep breath and my lungs filled with air. I wasn't dead yet. I was going to climb that hill. When they found me—if they found me—nobody would know whether I'd died trying or I'd lain down and given in and quit. But I'd know.

I started back up. The pitch became steeper and I used my hands to help my feet, dropping to all fours in places, climbing up as if my life really did depend on it. I didn't care what I'd find up there. All I knew was that I was going to reach the top, and if I found nothing, then maybe I'd have to climb to the next hill, and if that didn't bring me something, then the next hill. I had no guarantees other than the one that was certain if I stopped trying.

I reached the summit and tried to scream out in victory, but my voice came out cracked and hoarse and weak. Still, I was there. I hesitated for just a second before starting to look around, allowing myself one little moment of triumph before the certainty of defeat.

I gazed all around. I was high, higher than any other vantage point, and I could see in all directions. And in all directions there was nobody, nothing except the sand and rock and the sun getting ready to dip below the horizon. Yet in all that nothing, there was such a peace, a calm.

Without my realizing it, almost against my will, I was suddenly overwhelmed by the sheer beauty of the place. I took off my pack, set it down and sat on top of it, drinking in the surroundings. I watched as the sun turned orange and then red and sank into the sand, disappearing but leaving behind a warm, soft glow.

I pulled L'Orange of Tunisia out of my pocket. I didn't want to be alone. I wanted to share it with somebody else, especially a native Tunisian like L'Orange.

"Pretty amazing view," I said.

He didn't answer, which I took as a vote of agreement, as well as a sign that I still had limited sanity. If he had answered back, I would have been even more worried about that.

"People would pay big bucks to see something this beautiful, and neither of us paid a dime."

L'Orange didn't look impressed or unimpressed. He was very Zenlike that way. Although he'd shared the pleasant plumpness of Buddha in the beginning, he now looked as worn and shrivelled as I felt. There couldn't have been much liquid left inside of that orange peel. And then I thought that if there was any whatsoever, it would mean so much, it would taste so sweet.

I held L'Orange up higher so that he could see the sunset and I could see him more clearly. There had to be something still left in there ... something. But how could I even think about that? Wasn't it almost like cannibalism?

That was so *stupid*. This was just an orange, an orange that had been tossed out the window to me as a final insult. It was just an orange like all the others that had been bought and brought on this trip to eat.

I started to dig a fingernail into the peel and stopped myself. This *was* more than just an orange. L'Orange was my companion, one of the best friends I'd ever had. If Captain Evans asked me now who I'd never lied to, I'd at least have an answer—L'Orange of Tunisia. How pathetic was that? An orange was my best friend.

Really, though, even if it was my friend, it would want me to do what I needed to do so that I could survive. Didn't friends sacrifice for each other? Wasn't that what friendship was about? It was, I was certain. *Just eat the stupid orange,* I thought.

"I really appreciate you sacrificing yourself this way," I said. "Sorry, buddy."

I laughed—that was what Connor called me, "buddy." Connor probably had a lot of friends. He probably *deserved* to have a lot of friends.

I tucked L'Orange into my pocket. At least I could be a good friend at the end.

THE NIGHT TEMPERATURE had gone from a refreshing, wonderful, rewarding, valued cool to an uncomfortable cold. I pulled the sleeping bag a little tighter around my shoulders to ward off the chill. I was shaking. Was that a symptom of dehydration or the last little kick of my body suffering from alcohol withdrawal? I desperately could have used a drink right then, but for the first time in a long time, water would have been my preference.

I stood up and flicked the light on my headlamp. In the total darkness, it was amazing to me how far the beam extended. It lit a little path down the ridge right to the bottom. I played the light around in all directions, seeing everything that was to be seen—which of course was nothing.

I thought about how if I slowly spun around, I'd be like a little lighthouse, warning all ships out at sea not to get caught on the rocks of the ridge on which I sat. They called camels the ships of the desert. I guess my last efforts would be to provide safety for the camels. Maybe I'd even provide safety for the camels that led me astray. A final act of forgiveness.

I was guessing the little beam would be visible a long way off … and then it came to me. This light wouldn't just warn camels, it could make *me* visible! If Larson was out there looking for me and he saw this light, he'd have to know it was me. What else could it be? And if he saw the light, he'd come and find me. There was still life—there was still hope.

Slowly, ever so slowly, I started to turn around. I kept the beam as level as I could, not pointing up at the empty sky or down at the ground below, so that it would broadcast out into the night. I didn't know how far it would be seen, but I could see where the beam stopped being visible to me. That didn't mean anything, though, did it? I had to think.

I knew that I could see a light from a plane flying overhead at thousands of feet even if that light didn't exactly shine on me. I could see stars in the sky that were millions of miles away. So why couldn't somebody see this light from a few miles away? Of course they'd be able to see the light. But then again, the stars were gigantic balls of gas and the lights from the planes were brilliantly bright and big ... still ... in the darkness, it certainly seemed bright to me.

I continued to rotate on the spot. Not too quickly or I'd make myself dizzy, and not too slowly or it would take so long to rotate that they wouldn't be able to follow it, or they might just think their eyes were playing a little trick on them.

I let the sleeping bag fall to the sand. I wasn't feeling cold anymore. Maybe it was the motion, but more likely it was the heat of hope that was driving away the cold. The darkness, which I'd feared so much, was no longer my enemy—it was my friend, or if not a friend, at least an ally, working with me.

I was tired. My legs were sore and my feet hurt. My mouth felt dusty and dry, my throat was parched, and my whole body was crying out for water. Every muscle seemed to be close to the edge of exhaustion, and all I wanted to do was sit down, lie down, and stop moving. But I didn't. Like a good little lighthouse, I stood in place and slowly turned ... slowly turned ... slowly turned.

CHAPTER TWENTY-THREE

I STARTED, waking myself up again, and experienced a micro-second of panic when I didn't know where I was. Then waking up more fully, I fought off real panic. I couldn't waste any energy on panic. That was the twentieth time I'd fallen asleep, not standing and sleeping but spinning around and sleeping. Not walking in my sleep but rotating in my sleep.

As long as I was alert again, I decided to use the opportunity to change direction and rotate counter-clockwise for a while. I didn't know what time it was. I didn't know how long I'd been doing this. It had all become almost hypnotizing, mesmerizing, like that strange form of meditation that had made counting out my steps seem creative. My whole mind just went blank. Not thinking was refreshing, but now that I was back inside my head, I was starting to feel tired and thirsty again.

I remembered a conversation I'd had with Larson about how he could do the things he did. He'd told me about how you had to rise above your mind, to separate yourself from yourself so that you couldn't feel your body anymore, as if you were sitting or standing, or *floating,* above your own body and looking down at yourself. I needed to do that and allow my body to continue to be a good little lighthouse.

"Ethan."

Strange. My own name just popped into my head. Was this my body trying to keep my head connected to it, reminding me of who I was? Or was it L'Orange calling out encouragement from my pocket? He'd been silent up to that point, but maybe he was feeling dizzy and wanted me to stop.

"Ethan!"

My eyes popped open. That wasn't in my head. That was in my *ears*. I stopped rotating and listened. There was nothing except for the vague, soft whooshing of the wind. It might have just been the wind calling out to me. Was that a sign of insanity or was I simply in touch with my surroundings? Had all the inside-my-head sounds ceased and allowed me to hear the rhythm of the world around me?

"Ethan, can you hear me!"

It was faint but clear. That wasn't the wind—that was Larson.

"I hear …" My voice died, unable to make any sound except a low, crackling groan.

"Ethan, where are you!"

That was Andy's voice!

I turned and looked all around, searching for them, but I couldn't see anything. They must have seen my light, and now that I was standing still with the light shining down at the ground, they wouldn't be able to see it anymore.

"Ethan, can you hear me?" Larson yelled.

I struggled, trying to think: was his voice louder or softer? Were they coming closer or moving farther away, and which direction were the voices coming from?

I started to slowly spin again, hoping they could fix on the light and come to me. Even if I couldn't call them, at least they could see me, and the light would guide them toward me. If only I could call out.

My mouth felt bone dry. If I could work up some saliva to lubricate my vocal cords, I could yell out to them. I tried, straining to get some moisture into my mouth. If only there were just a few drops left in my water bottle or—there was L'Orange.

Like a strange animal, as if it weren't even connected to my mind, my hand crept down my side and into my pocket, pulling L'Orange free. He felt warm in my hand. Living, almost breathing. And inside his skin, inside that peel, was the little burst of moisture that would allow me to call out, allow them to find me. I didn't even have to eat all of him, just a section. How would that be different from an organ transplant, like a brother giving another brother his kidney? I'd do that for him. I'd give him a kidney if he needed one ... or a seed or two.

I'd try once more, first. I took a deep breath.

"I'm here!" I screamed, the loudness of my own voice surprising me, jarring me back to reality.

"I'm here! I'm here! I'm here!" I screamed.

I waited, unable to say anything more, and listened. Had they heard me? Had my voice travelled far enough?

"Ethan, we see you!" Larson yelled, and that was followed by a loud whooping sound that I knew had been made by Andy.

I saw a light come over the crest of another hill, another dune, and in that light I saw two figures moving through the sand.

"We see you, Ethan! Just stay there, keep your light on, and we'll come and get you!"

It was dreamlike, watching the two little bubbles of light that contained the two figures as they bobbled toward me and then disappeared behind another rise. I knew I should have been scared, or at least worried, as the light vanished, but I knew it would reappear. And then it did. They were getting closer and closer. They were starting up the hill.

I felt like crying, but I knew I couldn't. I didn't have enough moisture left for tears.

"Are you okay, Ethan?" Larson called out.

I nodded my head, and the light went up and down in response.

"Good. You just keep still and we'll be there!"

I wasn't going anywhere, even if I'd wanted to. I was so tired, so exhausted, so totally spent that I knew I didn't have the power left to rotate. Or even sit. Sitting seemed like too much work, and if I'd tried to lower myself to the ground, I'd probably either have collapsed or not had the strength to get back up again. As long as I was standing, I was alive. Dead people couldn't stand.

The lights started up the final section of the rise, and I turned slightly away as they caught me in their beams. I averted my light to the side so as to not blind them as well. I just stood waiting as they got closer and closer, the lights brighter and brighter until—

"Ethan, I'm so happy to see you," Larson said. He threw his arms around me, making me stagger backwards, almost knocking me off my feet. And then Andy threw his arms around both of us, stabilizing us all.

"Me too … thanks," I said softly. "Thanks to both of you for coming … but … but Connor and Kajsa? They're okay … right?"

"They're back at the camp," Larson said. "They're keeping a big bonfire going, hoping that you'll see it and find your way to us."

"Can't find anything," I whispered. "Too tired ... need some water."

"Oh, of course, here, take this!" Andy exclaimed.

He went to hand me a water bottle, but Larson took it from him.

"You can only have a sip first. Just a sip. Do you understand?"

"Understand."

"I'm going to pour it in your mouth. You need to swill it around in your mouth and then swallow it slowly. Okay?"

I nodded. I opened my mouth and he poured in some water. It splashed into my mouth and onto my face. It felt amazing, and I had to fight the urge to grab the bottle from his hand. Instead I swirled it around, letting it touch every part of my dry mouth, and tried to swallow it. My throat was so tight and dry that I gagged before it went down. It was unbelievable.

"That was ... heaven," I whispered.

"I'm going to give you the bottle now. Just drink it very slowly, okay?"

I nodded and took it. I held the bottle in my hand, looking at it, twirling it ever so slightly, watching as the water rolled around inside.

"Drink it," Larson said.

"Oh, yeah."

I'd forgotten, because looking at the water was so

wonderful. I tipped the bottle back and took another small sip. It went down much more easily.

"I have a lot of your stuff," Andy said.

"What?"

"The things from your pack that you left behind as you were walking. I've been gathering them up as we found them," he explained.

"That was brilliant," Larson said. "Marking a trail, like Hansel and Gretel."

"I just wish … wish I had some gingerbread right now."

They both laughed and I smiled.

"You were sick," I said to Andy.

"Still am."

"He wouldn't stay at the camp," Larson said. "He practically forced me to take him along."

"But … but why?"

"Because you were lost. Do you think eating half a goat and crapping it out the other end would stop the Terminator from finding his man?"

"You know about me calling you the Terminator?"

"Of course I do. I don't know if you meant it as a compliment, but that's the way I'm taking it. Good old Arnold is just about my favourite actor in the world. Can't understand why that man hasn't won an Oscar."

"Maybe because he can't act?" I whispered.

"Are you kidding? How many actors do you know who could play a cyborg?"

He did have a point.

"Do you think you can walk?" Larson asked.

"I can do whatever I need to do," I answered.

Andy bent down and started bundling up my sleeping bag. He stuffed it into the pack and then put in another armful of things that he'd been carrying as well.

"Thanks for doing that," I said. "Can you help me get it onto my back?"

"Are you an idiot?" he asked.

"I guess I deserve that. I am an idiot."

"Goes without saying," he replied. "Only an idiot would get himself lost out here."

"But you still came looking for me."

"You may be an idiot, but you're *our* idiot," Andy said.

"Come on now, slip one arm over my shoulder and the other around Andy's shoulders," Larson instructed.

"Why, do you two need my help to keep upright?" I asked.

"Something like that."

"How far do I have to walk?" I asked.

"Not far. Less than three kilometres," Larson said.

"But if you can't make it, don't worry. We'll carry you if we have to," Andy added.

I shook my head. "I can do it." I paused. "I can do anything now."

CHAPTER TWENTY-FOUR

MY EYES POPPED OPEN and what I saw was Connor's face staring right down at me. I nearly jumped out of my skin.

"I didn't mean to scare you like that. I was watching you sleep," he said.

I gave him a confused look.

"I know that sounds really creepy. We've been taking turns watching you sleep to make sure you're okay."

"I think I'm fine." I paused. "I just really have to pee."

"That's wonderful!" he exclaimed. He turned. "He's up and he's got to go to the washroom! He has to pee!" he yelled out the mesh of the tent.

Suddenly the door of the tent was filled with faces as Andy and Kajsa appeared.

"That's great news!" Kajsa said. "Just great!"

"Be sure to let us know what it looks like," Andy said firmly.

"You'll get a full written report, including quantity and quality," I said. "I'll provide it in triplicate."

"You better, or you will face the Terminator. *Hasta la vista*, baby."

I did a double take. That was an incredible impression. "Oscar quality, for sure."

Connor undid the tent zipper and I climbed out. I was surprisingly steady on my feet—which were sore, but not screaming out in pain.

"Here, drink this," Andy said as he handed me a water bottle.

"You don't understand. I'm trying to get rid of liquid."

"Drink," he said firmly.

I tipped back the bottle and drank, deep and long. My body was still crying out for liquids to replenish what I'd lost yesterday.

"Okay?" I asked.

"Okay," he replied and took the bottle back from me.

I went toward the edge of one of the buildings. Our camp was at the site of some ruins, on a rise, and sticking out of the dune were the tops and sides of a dozen stone buildings—thick walls, with openings where once there must have been doors or windows, but with most of the structures still buried beneath the sand.

Larson had told us about these buildings, about this settlement. As best as the historians could tell, they were well over five hundred years old, and at one time, long before living memory, the desert had simply swallowed them up. Then the relatives of the winds that had buried them in the first place blew away the sand, uncovering them again just a few years ago.

I couldn't help but think about the sands covering me up. Yesterday suddenly became more real again.

I gave a wide berth to the still smouldering embers of the bonfire that Kajsa and Connor had made to light the way back to camp. I could still see it burning in my mind. It was the biggest fire I'd ever seen in my life. If I hadn't been so tired, so exhausted, so nearly out of my head, I would have welcomed just sitting there. All I would have needed were a few marshmallows.

I rounded the corner and, now out of sight, started to pee. It flowed out, dark yellow, but still yellow. It kept coming and coming and coming. If this was a sign that I was rehydrated, then I was rehydrated. I figured I should be. I'd drunk gallons of water before I'd finally drifted off, and then Larson had woken me repeatedly throughout the night and forced me to drink more water than I thought I could hold.

"That looks good."

I turned slightly at the sound of Larson's voice.

"You know, a week ago I would have called the police if some guy snuck up behind me and told me that my urine looked good."

"A week ago was a lifetime ago."

"More bumper sticker sayings?" I asked.

"It sounds like I should get myself a car."

The flow stopped and I zipped up. "You don't have a car?" I asked in amazement. "Next thing you're going to tell me is that you drive a camel."

"I have many camels." He paused. "Not to sound like I'm bragging or anything."

I laughed. "Camel envy isn't one of my many faults."

"I don't know about faults, but your kidneys must be made out of steel to have survived so well."

"My kidneys are good, but I woke up with a splitting headache this morning. I feel the way I used to after staying up drinking all night—like a hangover."

"That's a dehydration symptom—alcohol causes it, too. We'll just keep giving you lots of water today."

"Do we have lots of water?" I asked.

"We have as much as you can drink. We're all going to cut down on our intake to make sure you have enough."

"You don't have to do that."

"Actually we do. I've got to tell you, I'm pretty impressed by what you did."

"You're impressed with the fact that I got lost in the desert and almost died?"

"I'm impressed you got lost in the desert and *didn't*

die. I've known people who've lived their whole lives here who got lost and panicked."

"I think I was too scared to panic."

"No, I'm serious. You were so calm."

"If calm is another word for nearly catatonic, then I was calm. In fact, other than dying, I couldn't have gotten any calmer."

"Don't sell yourself short. You *should* have been scared, but you still did everything right, including leaving a trail of your belongings for us to follow."

I thought about claiming that as part of my master plan, but I just couldn't bring myself to do it.

"You're thinking I was smarter than I was. I was leaving things behind because I was trying to lighten my pack. You're giving me more credit than I deserve."

"Now I'm even more impressed. You could have left me with the wrong impression, but you didn't. There's a lot more to you than you give yourself credit for. A lot more than your father knows about."

"Are you planning on telling him that?"

"No need. You'll be showing him yourself as time passes." He smiled. "But enough about the future. We need to live in the moment. We're all just grateful to have you back."

"Especially you. I imagine my father wouldn't have paid you if I died."

"Ethan, your life means more than a few dollars."

"I'm sure he paid you more than a few dollars."

"He did, and the money has already been delivered. It's mine whether you live or die, although I have a preference."

"So do I."

"You know this has to be about more than money, or it isn't about anything," he said.

"My father wouldn't agree with that."

"He's entitled to his opinion ... even when he's wrong."

"I don't think my father would ever admit to being wrong, and I guess, if making money shows you know what you're doing, then he's wrong less than almost anybody on the whole planet."

"It isn't all about making money."

"But you certainly were willing to accept money to take me, and the others, on this trek."

"Money is not intrinsically good or bad. It's what it's used for that *makes* it good or bad," he said.

"And just what *good and noble* thing are you going to use this money for?" I asked.

"Water."

"You're going to buy water?" In some ways, after yesterday, that didn't seem like such a strange thing to spend money on.

"Not really buy the water. I get the money to dig wells so that water can come to the surface."

"Wells ... how many wells do you have?"

"Not enough."

"Cute answer. How many do you have?" I asked again.

"I've been able to raise enough funds to build seven wells."

"And you need an eighth?"

"An eighth and a ninth and a tenth and an eleventh and ... well, you get the idea."

I could understand the need for a well and water maybe better than anybody in the entire world right now, but why would anyone need to build so many wells ... unless ...

"You put in that well at the oasis where we stayed the other night, didn't you?"

"Why would you think that?"

"It was something the nomads said to Kajsa."

"I don't know how much Arabic she knows, but she probably just misunderstood."

"She doesn't speak any Arabic, but she was managing to communicate pretty well in French, and she got more answers than you're giving me. That well is yours, isn't it?"

"Nobody owns a well, it's for all."

"You're still not answering my question."

"I didn't dig the well."

I let out a big sigh of frustration. "Did you or did you not provide the money for that well to be dug?"

He nodded his head ever so slightly.

"Now, was that so hard?"

"Not hard. Just not something I talk much about," he admitted.

"And that's why you do this, why you take people on these little strolls through the desert, so you can get money to have wells dug?"

"I do this for lots of different reasons, but the money allows me to help in my own small way."

"So what are you trying to do, put in wells across the whole desert?" I joked.

"Yes, I am," he said quietly.

I laughed.

"No, really." He paused. "But that's enough about me for now. What's important is about you, and what's going to happen today."

"What's going to happen?"

"We're going to walk to the next oasis and then rest."

"How far is that?" I asked.

"Less than fifteen kilometres. Do you think you can walk that far?"

"I can walk that far. How far is Tunis?"

"Just over one hundred kilometres."

"But I have to be there in two days!"

"I'm afraid that's not going to happen."

"It *has* to happen!"

"I'm sorry, I really am. I know you'll lose money but—"

"This isn't about the money."

He looked confused. "Is this about showing your father that you can do it?"

I shook my head. "It's about me. I'm going to get there … in two days."

"Do you have any idea how hard it is to travel a hundred kilometres in two days?"

"No, but you do. Is it possible?"

"Of course it's possible. I've done it."

"But can we?"

"That's certainly a question."

"Then I guess the only other question is whether or not you're going to help me get there." I paused. "Well?"

He looked at his watch. "We'd better get going."

CHAPTER TWENTY-FIVE

THERE WAS A CERTAIN SENSE of satisfaction in travelling so far so quickly, and so early in the morning. There was also a certain level of smartness. The sun was still low in the sky, and we'd been moving for two and a half hours. In that time we'd stopped, briefly, only twice. Both times it was for Kajsa's bathroom breaks, and both times she had insisted that we do a double-time march for a minute afterwards to make up the time and distance she'd cost us.

Larson had made it clear to me that if we were going to make a big push to get to Tunis, it would have to be something we all agreed on. So we sat down together to discuss it. Andy was up for it immediately—he was always ready to push himself a little harder—and Connor and Kajsa signed on, too. Even though nobody said this out loud, I know we all understood that if anyone struggled, if anyone changed their mind, we would simply slow down again or take a break if we had to. Maybe, I thought, that was what being a team was really about—not just the obnoxious rah-rah, go-team kind of stuff. It was about real, mutual respect.

Larson led the way, setting the pace, and we followed behind, sometimes in pairs, sometimes four across, sometimes in single file, but always matching and meeting the rhythm he was setting with his feet. I broke into a little jog so that I could catch up to him.

"Hey, how far have we gone?" I asked.

"Remember when I told you there was an oasis about fifteen kilometres from where we started?"

"Yeah?"

"Look up."

There on the horizon was the oasis!

"I feel like I'm looking at a mirage," I said.

"It's real. We did fifteen kilometres in under three hours."

"So if we moved at this pace for twelve hours, we could cover sixty kilometres today?"

"That's the mathematical answer. The physiological answer is different. If you tried to keep up this pace right through the middle of the day, you'd break down."

"I'm not going to break down."

"Somebody is. The thing about pacing yourself is that you find a rhythm that your body can keep, you find your limit."

"But what if we push past that rhythm, past the limit? I know you've done that."

"I've spent the better part of my life trying to make impossible into possible," he said.

"If you could do it for a lifetime, why don't you think we can do it for two days?" I demanded.

"I didn't say you couldn't. I'm not here to stop you. I'm here to lead you. I'll let you push as hard as you can push. But right now, we have to slow the pace."

"But you just said that—"

"That I'm here to lead you. I've done this a couple of times before. I know how to do it. We slow down the pace and relax the muscles so that after we stop at the oasis for our break, we can get started again. Of course, if you really want to go off by yourself again, you're welcome to do that."

"I get the message."

We kept walking—at a slower pace, step after step—but the oasis was elusively, annoyingly farther than I'd originally thought. Distances in the desert can be like that. I kept my eyes on it, making sure it wasn't going to disappear like some mirage. As we got closer, I started to make out its individual features. There was scrub brush and bushes and trees, although none of the trees seemed very tall. I thought I could pick out water, but the intensity of the heat often made the overheated air wave so that it appeared to shimmer like water.

"Is this well yours, too?" I asked.

"None of the wells are mine."

"Are we going to go through this again?"

"I provided the funds for this one, yes. It's the newest."

"I thought so. The trees aren't that big."

"But the water is sweet. Can you smell it?"

"Water doesn't have a smell."

"Yes, it does. Try."

I was going to argue, but arguing about the smell of water made less sense than thinking it had a smell to begin with. I inhaled deeply through my nose. All I caught was a whiff of concentrated heat.

"How long are we going to stay at the oasis?" I asked.

"Not long. We'll refill our water containers, soak our feet, grab something to eat and have a nap in the shade."

"We don't have time for a nap! We have too far to travel today!" I exclaimed.

"Because we have so far to travel, we need to take a nap."

"There's no way I can sleep," I said.

"You don't have to sleep, but you do need to stay in the shade and out of the noonday sun and heat. It takes too much out of you to travel during that time."

"But if we don't travel all day, there's no way we can put in the miles!" I protested.

"We'll start moving by two."

"That means we'll have less than five hours before dark. We can't cover thirty-five kilometres in that time."

"You're right, we can't. That's why we won't be stopping at sundown."

"We're going to walk in the dark?"

"We'll move as far as the four of you can travel. But first things first. Let's get to the oasis."

TWO OF THE SLEEPING BAGS had been opened and strung between trees to provide shade. It was still unbelievably hot, but much cooler than in the open. The five of us crowded into that little space. There was hardly any conversation, and the only words spoken were in hushed tones, so as not to wake up anybody who'd managed to get to sleep. Everyone, including me, had slept for at least a little while, but Larson seemed to be napping for almost the whole rest time. He'd eaten, drunk some water, lain down and gone to sleep.

I looked at my watch. It was almost two. Somebody was going to have to wake him up soon or we'd miss our restart time.

Almost on cue, he sat up. Everybody looked at him. "It's time," he said.

Those two words seemed to energize us. Everybody began to put on their socks and shoes.

Mine were already on—I'd been afraid to take them off. I got up and started to take down our shelter, undoing the strings to free up the sleeping bags.

The gear was all stowed back inside our packs and the water bottles were topped up to the very limit. We were ready to go.

"Okay, let's get moving," Larson said.

CONNOR SLOWED HIS PACE until he was right beside me.

"Can we talk?" he asked quietly.

"Of course."

"In private?"

"Yeah, of course."

We both slowed down a little more so that the other three moved farther ahead and out of hearing distance. I had a pretty good idea what he wanted to talk about and was already feeling guilty. I had to say something—should I come clean about the whole thing?

"I wanted to talk to you about Ashley," he said.

"I thought you might. I was just—"

"I really want to thank you."

"You don't need to thank me for—"

"I know, I know, friends don't have to thank friends, but still, I want to. It's not just about Ashley, it's about how I pretend that things that bother me don't bother me."

"I'm not sure how much she really is still bothering you."

"She's not. Not now. I did what you said. I thought about the whole situation and realized that I was right in breaking up with her."

"But I thought she broke *your* heart?"

"Well, she did. It just hurt me so much to have to break up with her. I felt like such a jerk, but I had to do it. It was the right thing, and because of you, I can put all of that away, and that's why I'm thanking you."

I thought about confessing, but what was the point?

"Well, then, you're welcome."

I was glad he felt better. I knew I did. Maybe that wasn't the most honest resolution, but it was the best for him, and that made it the best for me.

"How far do you think we've gone already today?" Connor asked.

I could have told him in steps, but he might have found that a little freaky.

"We did fifteen kilometres before the break and now another eighteen after, so about thirty-three kilometres."

"Any other time that would seem like a pretty amazing distance," he commented.

"Not today. We're basically just two-thirds of the way to our goal."

"Do you really think we can do fifty kilometres?" he asked.

"Not before dark, but we'll do it. How are you feeling?"

"I'm good, but I'm worried about Kajsa. She looks tired," Connor replied.

I'd been watching her for the last few kilometres and noticed that she was struggling. Her stride was shorter, and more choppy.

"She's tough. She won't stop," I said.

"If worst comes to worst, we'll just have Andy carry her on his back. I think he could walk all the way to Tunis tonight," Connor said.

"Always good to have the Terminator on your side."

Up ahead the three of them came to a stop. Kajsa slipped off her pack and went off to the side once again. As she disappeared behind a slight ridge, we caught up with Andy and Larson.

"How about if you all go ahead. I'll wait for her," I offered.

"I can wait, too," Connor added.

"All of us can wait," Andy said.

I shook my head and smiled. "You know you want to keep going," I said to Andy. "All of you keep going and we'll catch up. I promise."

"Okay," Larson said, "but don't get lost."

"Yeah, or this time we're not going to come looking for you," Andy said.

"I won't get lost. Just get going."

They all started back into gear. I slipped off my pack and set it down beside Kajsa's. I undid the zipper and went to pull out my extra water bottle when I had another thought. I undid Kajsa's zipper and started removing things from her pack. I took out her sleeping bag and the tent and put them into my pack. I'd have to do this fast before she reappeared because she might object if she knew what I was doing.

Next I grabbed her headlamp, some clothes and an extra pair of shoes. I stuffed them in and then, with a struggle, did up the zipper. I zippered her pack up again, just as she reappeared. She hadn't seen anything.

"Sorry, I feel like I'm slowing everybody down," she apologized.

"You're not slowing anybody down." I gestured to the three of them, still within sight.

"How about you?" she asked.

"I had to stop to go to the washroom myself," I said. A little white lie. "I told them not to wait because we'd catch them."

I reached down and grabbed her pack. It did feel light.

"Here you go," I said as I started to help her put it back on.

She slipped her arms into the harnesses. "Strange … it feels lighter."

"That's probably just because you've rested for a minute ... and lost all that weight out of your bladder," I offered as an excuse.

"Not much weight lost from the walnut-sized bladder. I'm really going to have to have somebody look at it when I get back."

"It wouldn't hurt," I said, "but I'm sure it's nothing. You said you've always been like this, and your doctor did do tests, right?"

"Lots of them."

"And he found nothing, so don't worry."

"It's kind of you to say that," she said. "I know you're just trying to make me feel better."

"No, I'm not," I argued. "I hardly ever say anything to try to make anybody feel better." That was certainly the truth. "Just don't worry is all I'm saying. Everything is going to be fine."

"Thank you."

She reached over and, to my complete shock, gave me a little kiss on the cheek!

"You and Connor and Andy have been so good to me ... you're all like my brothers!" she exclaimed.

That took away any possible confusion around what that kiss meant, but really, she *was* like my sister.

"Now, let's catch up to them," I said.

"No, let's not just catch them," she replied, "let's get in front of them!"

THE SUN HAD DIPPED DOWN so low that the hills and dunes cast shadows, some long enough for us to hide in. There was still at least thirty minutes before it disappeared completely, and another fifteen minutes after that when there'd still be light. There wasn't a cloud in the sky, so we'd eventually have the light from the stars and moon to help show us the way.

I did a mental update of the distance we'd travelled as I counted off another thousand steps: forty-six kilometres. That was at least four kilometres more than I'd ever walked before—and except for Larson, four kilometres more than any of us had ever gone. Even Andy, that marathon-running, cross-country-biking cyborg, had never gone this far before.

We were, officially, doing an ultra-marathon, with another nine kilometres still to go to reach the halfway mark in our two-day trek to Tunis. Nine kilometres, nine thousand steps, an hour and a half of walking, and the day would be over.

We were still moving together, but no longer beside each other. Larson led, followed by Andy a few strides behind. Next, much farther back, was Connor, and Kajsa was right on his tail. I was bringing up the rear. I could have kicked a little harder and caught them, but I liked being in the back. It was reassuring to see them all in front of me. And it was a good place to be if you wanted to count steps, think, or talk to yourself, and I was doing a lot of all three.

When this had all started, I was too angry and shocked to even begin to think about anything, including what I was going to do when I reached Tunis. It hadn't been real enough to warrant thinking about my future when every ounce of my energy was needed just to survive the present. Now, still a day's distance away, it was more real. What was I going to do when I got there?

The first couple of steps were no-brainers. I was going to the lawyer's office to collect the money. Next, I was going to have a big, cold, long, bottomless drink ... of water. Whatever steps came next—and those were the ones I wasn't sure of—needed to be made with a clear, sober mind. I wasn't going to commit to giving up drinking, but that was definitely something I could think about later. If I was going to drink, that, like everything, was my decision to make.

The first option was the simplest. Get on a plane, fly home and see my father. I just didn't know if I should, or could, do that. First off, was it really my home? Second, even when I got there, what would I say to him? Would he expect me to thank him, or break down in tears, or apologize? Because I wasn't ready for any of those. Or would we just fall into the old dynamic, with him putting me aside and me trying to force him to see me? Would we slide into the same pattern of anger, annoyance and avoidance? Because if that happened, all of this had meant nothing. And it had to mean *something*.

I needed to talk, and there was only one person I wanted to talk to.

I pulled L'Orange out of my pocket. He was not looking well. He'd lost a lot of weight and was much more oval than round. His orange peel was still bright, but it was cracked and creased. I would have said something about how he was letting himself go, but who was I to talk? I was unwashed, sweat soaked, smelly beyond belief, and my feet were pulp. I guess, relatively speaking, L'Orange was in fine shape.

"So, L'Orange, have you ever been to New York?"

No answer.

"I didn't think so. We have many, many fine oranges in the States, although mainly from California and Florida ... not so many in New York. We could go to one of those states instead. In fact, we could go anywhere in the entire world! Any thoughts? Is there any place you've always wanted to go, a place you have a passion for?"

Still no answer, but I understood. Where did *I* have a passion to go?

"Come on, I'd really like some feedback. After all we've been through, I really want to know what you have on your mind. You must have an opinion."

"Ethan?"

For a split second, I thought it was L'Orange answering before I looked up to see Larson standing there, staring at me.

"That's quite the conversation you were having with yourself," he said.

"I wasn't talking to myself. I was discussing things with my friend L'Orange of Tunisia," I blurted out. I held out L'Orange for him to see.

He looked confused, then amused. He reached out his hand as though he was going to take L'Orange away!

"Very pleased to meet you, Monsieur L'Orange," he said as he shook my hand—L'Orange's hand!

"He's not much for conversation, but he's pleased to meet you, too," I said.

"Just because he doesn't answer doesn't mean he isn't part of the conversation," Larson said. "Sorry for interrupting. It sounded serious."

"Very. Just trying to decide what I'm going to do when I reach Tunis."

"That *is* important. If you're looking for another opinion, I think I have an apple in my pack," Larson offered.

I couldn't help but laugh.

"I'll let you get back to your discussion. I was just checking to see how you were doing," he said.

"I'm having a lively conversation with an orange. How well do you think I'm doing?" I asked.

"Without trying to offend you, a lot better than I expected."

"I'm not offended. I am doing a lot better than I thought."

"A few days into this, I was starting to feel bad for you," Larson said. "This whole thing, the shock of being here, the fact that you didn't want to be here, and really the complete lack of training. There was no way you should have been able to do this."

"I *am* going to do this," I said quietly.

"I know you are, and whether you think this is stupid or not, I'm proud of what you've done."

I wanted to tell him it was stupid, to yell out that it wasn't fair, to tell him that crossing a desert wasn't anything to be proud of. I didn't.

"Thanks," I said. "That means a lot, especially coming from you. But then again, until we reach Tunis, I haven't done anything."

"If you stopped right now and didn't walk another step, you'd have done something."

I shook my head. "Something would have been getting to Tunis and getting there earlier than we were supposed to."

"Do you think that would impress your father?"

"I'm not trying to impress him or anybody else. I'm just trying to get to Tunis ... and the sooner, the better. There is something about pushing harder than you've ever pushed before ... and then pushing even *harder*."

Larson smiled. "To do that, all we have to do is keep walking. Are you and your orange up to that?"

"We can go as long as we need to go."

"Okay, and to keep walking, we all need to get closer together and put on our headlamps," Larson suggested.

Headlamps ... I had two in my pack.

"Then I guess we'd better catch up to the others. I have some of Kajsa's stuff in my pack, including her headlamp."

"How did that happen?" he asked.

"Earlier today when she was struggling, I rearranged some things out of her bag while she was off relieving herself."

"Does she know you did that?"

I shook my head. "I knew she'd just say no if I asked, and I figured she really needed a little help. The way she and Connor took some of Andy's stuff when he was so sick."

I was suddenly feeling guilty, as though I'd stolen from her. "I didn't do anything wrong ... did I?"

"I guess it depends on why you did it," he said.

"I don't understand."

"Did you take her things because you were worried she was going to slow us down and cost you money, or because you saw a friend who needed your help and would have been too proud to ask for it?"

"Even if I told you, you wouldn't believe me."

"I wouldn't have believed you seven days ago," he replied.

"And you think that somehow my walking across the desert has changed me *so* much?"

"Actually, I don't think it's changed you at all," he said.

"Really?" I gasped. After all this, how could he not think it had had any impact?

"This experience hasn't *changed* who you are. It has simply *revealed* who you are." He smiled. "How's that for a bumper sticker?"

I relaxed enough then to give him a smile. "I'd put that on my car … or my camel."

"As would I. So, answer the question, why did you do it?"

"It isn't about the money," I said. "I'm not sure when or why that changed, but it just isn't anymore."

"Then why?"

"To help," I said quietly. "I was just trying to be a friend … I saw that she needed help and I was there to offer it … the way I know she would have offered to help me. I guess I haven't had much practice with this friend thing."

"That's okay," he said, and then he smiled and put an arm around my shoulders. "You'll have plenty of time to practise in the years to come."

CHAPTER TWENTY-SIX

WE MOVED IN A TIGHT LITTLE FORMATION, with Larson leading, Kajsa and me tight behind, and Andy and Connor in a pair right on our tails. We were so close that the beams from all five headlamps blurred together into one patch of light. Larson had insisted that we stay this close, but I really didn't think we needed much encouragement. Being together, in the light, gave us a feeling of safety. Alone out there was eerie. I knew that from experience, but I think the others just instinctively knew it. Of course, Larson's explanation that when the sun went down, other things came out—vipers and scorpions and bugs that bite—hadn't hurt the cause.

Kajsa wasn't angry at me when she found out. She gave me another kiss on the cheek. She did, however, insist on taking back all her things. She wanted to carry her "own weight." She even tried to convince me that she should take a couple of things out of *my* pack to make it up to me. I said no way, and I noticed that she didn't fight too hard.

There was something very, very different about travelling in the dark. It wasn't just that we were free of the sun and it was much cooler—although those facts were refreshingly wonderful. It was what we could see—or, to be more accurate, what we couldn't see. Our entire world seemed to be no bigger than the width and length of the throw of our headlamps. There was a whole world out there, but for us, it wasn't real. All that was real was a bobbing, travelling patch of light and the five people walking within it.

Larson stopped and we all instantly came to a halt. He held up his hand, and in unison, without the need for words, we all responded by turning off our lights. It instantly became jet black, and then, as our eyes began to adjust, we could see. Up in the sky the stars began to reappear—not that they hadn't been there, but now they were revealed ... sort of like what Larson had said about me. They were always up there, above New York or London or Paris, just the same as they were above the desert. Sometimes you just couldn't see them.

And right now, Larson needed to see them. He was using the stars to navigate, to show us the way we had to travel. We'd stopped like this five times already. That was the only thing I'd been counting. I didn't know how many steps we'd travelled, and I didn't even want to look at my watch.

"Congratulations," Larson said, breaking the silence.

"We're here?" Connor asked. "We've done it?"

"We've done it. We've travelled fifty-five kilometres today."

There was a chorus of cheers and a slapping of backs, and everybody in turn gave everybody else—including me—a hug.

"But how can you be so sure?" I asked.

"I know this spot. I just needed my eyes to adjust enough to recognize it. We're at the halfway mark. We went fifty-five kilometres today and we have fifty-five left to travel tomorrow. Let's set up camp and—"

"What if we *don't* set up camp?" I asked.

"We're here," Larson said. "We've reached our goal for the day."

"An amazing goal!" Connor exclaimed.

"It is amazing," Larson said. "I've never had anybody travel this far in one day before."

I took two steps farther along the trail. "I'm just saying … why are we stopping right now?"

"We have to stop somewhere," Larson said, "unless you're planning on walking all the way to Tunis tonight."

"No, of course not. That would be impossible. But why stop right here, right now? I can go a little bit farther. Can other people?"

"I'm good to go," Andy said.

I knew I could count on him.

"I could go a bit farther," Kajsa said, and Connor nodded along in agreement.

"I'm just thinking that any step we take tonight is a step we don't have to take tomorrow," I said. "And right now, I still have some steps in me." I paused. "I really don't want to just stand here and talk about it. Standing is so hard on the knees. Could we at least walk a little and talk about it while we're walking?"

"It's not up to me," Larson said. "What do you four want to do?"

"All in favour of walking a bit farther?" Andy said, and he held up his hand as if he was voting. Three other hands joined his.

And just like that, we started walking again into the night.

"ETHAN ... WAKE UP."

I was startled ever so slightly, but came back to reality quickly. I got to my feet and flicked on my headlamp, and the sleeping bag that had been wrapped around my shoulders dropped to the ground. I picked it up and stuffed it back into my pack. The others were doing the same.

"How long were we out?" I asked.

"Fifteen minutes," Larson answered.

"That was longer than the last time," I mumbled.

"That was longer than all the times before, but you needed it. You all needed it."

Dreamily I nodded my head. We'd been moving along in the darkness, hardly exchanging a word, and then Larson would stop and tell us to sleep for a few minutes. Then, again without words, we'd slump to the ground, pull out a sleeping bag and go to sleep. Deep, instant sleep. Funny, but there were no dreams when I was actually sleeping, even though I felt that strange, dreamy quality when I was awake.

"Everybody grab some food," Larson said.

"I'm not hungry," I mumbled.

"I wasn't asking if you were hungry. Eat."

He passed around a package of cookies and we all pulled out a few. Almost instantly I felt a rush of chocolate and sugar and carbs go surging through my body.

"How long is it before the sun comes up?" Connor asked.

"About three hours," Larson said.

That meant it was about three-thirty in the morning. That meant we'd started walking almost *twenty* hours ago.

"How far?"

"Tunis is somewhere between fifteen and twenty kilometres away."

"Can we do it?" I asked.

"You could go to sleep right now and sleep in until two in the afternoon, and we'd still be there before sunset, right on schedule. Of course you can do it."

"No, no, you don't understand. Can we do it before sunrise? I don't want to be there when we're supposed to be there. I want to be there *before* we're supposed to be there … that would be something."

Larson let his light pass from person to person, illuminating their faces. It was almost scary to see. Each looked so drawn and drained, with only their eyes animated, looking wild and bright.

"Well, can we do it … do you all want to try?" Larson asked.

"That which does not kill us makes us stronger," I said.

Andy chuckled. "Friedrich Nietzsche."

"This won't actually kill us, will it?" Kajsa asked.

Larson shook his head. "You might not be able to walk again for a week afterwards, but it won't kill you."

"I'm not going to *want* to walk again for more than a week," Connor joked. "But … but I'm in. I'm not ready to stop. We all came here to push our limits, so why stop now?"

"I agree," Andy said. "Fifteen kilometres is nothing."

"I'm in, too," Kajsa said.

I turned to Larson. "So we all want to try."

"Okay, then that's what we're going to do," he said. "Except for one thing." He paused and we all waited. "Do or do not … there is no try."

"Hold it," Andy said, "isn't that from *Star Wars*?"

Larson looked embarrassed.

"Great, we've gone from Nietzsche to Yoda in less than one minute," I said.

"Both very wise philosophers," Larson remarked. "But there is one more thing you have to do. Take off your packs."

We all hesitated for a second, and then we peeled them off our backs and let them settle to the ground. I felt—literally and figuratively—as though a weight had been taken off me. I almost felt taller.

"There's nothing in those we're going to need tonight. Tomorrow I'll send somebody back to get them. We've finished the marathon … we've finished more than *two* marathons. Now it's time for the sprint to the finish."

AT FIRST, not carrying the packs had been like getting a massive burst of energy. I'd felt so light, so free, that I was practically flying. In the beginning I almost had to fight the urge to run or skip, but those feelings quickly drained away. Then, without our packs, we were left with no choice. We couldn't stop even if we wanted to. There were no sleeping bags to provide warmth, no tents for shelter, no pots for cooking, no nothing for anything. After a while, not having a choice was probably the only thing that kept us moving forward.

Andy tipped back his water bottle and drained the last little bit, even tapping it with his finger to get that last drop. "That's the end of it," he said.

"I have a bit left." Kajsa held up a bottle with no more than a few ounces of liquid.

"I'm dry," Connor added. "Ethan?"

"Gone. Larson?" I asked.

"None left."

I thought about it and realized that he'd been telling us to drink and watched as we'd consumed the last of our water, but I hadn't actually noticed him drinking anything.

"When was the last time you had any water?" I asked him.

"I've been drinking."

"And your urine … is it good?" I asked.

Everybody burst into laughter.

"Don't you think that's a little personal?" he asked.

"Kajsa?" I asked. "I think he needs the last of the water."

She passed the bottle to me and I passed it to Larson. "No arguing."

"Yes, sir," he said and gave me a little salute. He hesitated for a second, and then put the bottle to his lips and drank down the last few ounces.

"It's getting lighter," Connor said.

"The sun will be up soon."

"But we're not there … we're not going to … what's that sound?" I asked.

"I hear it too," Connor said. "It's like the ocean or the wind."

It sounded so familiar, but it wasn't the wind.

"It's traffic," Larson said.

"There's no traffic in the … is there a road?" I asked.

"Just over this dune is the main highway … the one that leads right into Tunis."

Without another word, we all started moving. The dune was big and the sand was soft and sliding backwards. I tripped forward, and both Connor and Kajsa grabbed hold, hauling me back to my feet. Together we scrambled higher and higher, and just before we reached the crest, the first rays of sunlight peeked over the dune.

We clambered up to the top and stopped, frozen by the sight.

The sun was rising up out of the ocean, bright and red and blazing. In its light, stretching out before us, was a city. There were houses and tall buildings, roads and highways, stores and cars and people and … we'd done it. We'd reached Tunis!

CHAPTER TWENTY-SEVEN

WE WERE ALL SITTING under an umbrella at one of the endless sidewalk cafés that lined the main thoroughfare of Tunis. The road was filled with traffic and the sidewalk crowded with pedestrians, and it reminded me a lot of the Champs-Élysées in Paris. It was a big, modern, beautiful city, home to hundreds of thousands of people, filled with cars and restaurants and stores, with paved roads, electricity and running water … water … I took another sip and finished the bottle.

"Waiter!" I called out. "Another round for my friends!"

"Are you sure you need anything else to drink?" Connor asked.

I burst out laughing. "I've had people say that to me before, but never when there was nothing but water on the table."

"You know you can get drunk on water," Andy said.

"Then I am totally drunk!"

"I'm serious. The condition is called hyper-hydration. If a person were to consume gallons and gallons of water, his electrolyte levels would become dangerously low and—"

"I'm not going to drink *that* much water!" I protested.

"I know," he said, and smiled. "Just giving you a hard time ... the way you were giving me a hard time about my knees. I knew you were just joking around."

"That's me, always joking," I said.

The waiter put down four more bottles of water.

"I propose a toast," I said.

I lifted up my bottle, as did Connor, Kajsa and Andy.

"A toast for making the walk, beating the time and being a great team!"

"Team?" Kajsa asked. "I don't see any *uniforms.*"

"And I didn't sign up to be any part of any *team,*" Connor joked.

I smiled. "You guys aren't going to let me forget what I said, are you?"

"I don't think any of us are going to forget any part of this," Andy said. "But let's give the guy a break. He *is* part of the team." He paused. "Sort of like the mascot."

"To the team!" I called out, and we all clinked bottles and took a sip of water.

Kajsa got to her feet. "Water in, water out."

She hobbled away on sore, bandaged feet. We all had sore, bandaged feet. Even the Terminator … even *Larson* had blisters. That walk—that hundred and ten kilometres in twenty-four hours, our ultra-double marathon—had worn down even Larson a bit.

"So what are you going to do with all your money?" Andy asked.

"Isn't that obvious? I'm going to buy lots and lots of water."

"And after that?" Connor questioned.

"After that, I can't tell you for sure."

"Well, one thing you'd better do is keep in touch. You got that, buddy?"

"I got that, buddy," I agreed, and I meant it … both parts. I would stay in touch, and he was my buddy. They were all my buddies. "It's a promise."

I reached out to offer my hand to shake. Connor took it, and then Andy put his hand on top of both of ours.

"You'd better keep your word," he said, suddenly looking serious and scary, "or *I'll be back*."

His Arnold impression—as always—was perfect, but it wasn't the impression that I was thinking about so much as the words: *I'll be back*.

I caught sight of Larson as he came out the front door of the hotel where we were staying. He waved and then yelled. "Andy! Connor! They've made the telephone connections ... we have a line to both of your families!"

Kajsa had already spoken to her family, but then there had been problems getting through and neither of the guys had had the chance. They both jumped excitedly to their feet and then hesitated.

"Why don't you go?" Connor said to Andy. "I'll talk to my parents after."

"Don't worry," I said. "I think I'll be fine on my own for a few minutes. Remember, I was lost in the desert by myself and I survived."

"Barely," Andy noted. "You have to promise not to wander off."

"Promise. Besides, here I have water. In fact, don't expect *your* water to be here when you get back."

"I'm not sure you want mine," Andy said. "Lots of backwash."

"Great. I'll order another." I paused. "Say hello to your parents, and tell your father that trip, that bike trip you two took, that was really ... really something."

Andy smiled. "I'll tell him."

Andy left, and Connor hesitated again.

"Get moving. Say hello to your parents as well, okay?"

"Okay, I'll say hello, but I'm expecting you to say that in person before too much longer. You are coming for a visit, right?"

"Wouldn't miss it. I just can't promise right away."

He nodded and, of course, smiled. Then he raced off to catch up to Andy. Both gave Larson a high-five as they ran by.

Larson started toward me. It would be just the two of us. I'd been looking forward to that. And dreading it. He pulled up a seat.

"How are you doing?"

"I'm doing well. How about you, how are *your* feet?" I asked.

"They're still sore, but thanks for asking. And thanks for pushing us all to do more."

"Yeah, right, like you needed to be pushed," I joked.

"Maybe pushed isn't the right word. How about inspired?"

"That makes even less sense. I've inspired a guy who's climbed the highest mountains and run across the whole desert?"

"What you've done at your age is pretty remarkable."

"Most of the things I've done I'd like to forget," I said.

"No!" he exclaimed, and the intensity of his response caught me off guard. "Forget nothing, regret nothing, because it's all part of who you are."

"That is way too long for a bumper sticker, you realize that, don't you?"

"That's a wraparound," he said, gesturing in a circle. "Right around the whole camel. But I mean what I said. You've already got some things figured out that I didn't understand until I was decades older than you."

"But I don't know where I'm going to go or what I'm going to do, so how is that understanding anything?"

"The fact that you know that puts you miles ahead of almost everybody else. You were lost."

"I'm *still* lost."

"Nope, you're not lost," he said. "You just haven't found what you're looking for … yet … but you will."

"I wish I could be so sure about that."

"I'm sure. Just don't make the mistake I made," he said.

"Don't worry, there's no danger I'm going to have my toenails removed."

"Don't you ever stop joking around?" he asked.

"Not usually. Besides, I'm drunk on water, or maybe high on life. So what mistake *did* you make?"

"I thought moving was progress. For years, for decades, I didn't realize that you can run in place, run in circles, run away or run in the wrong direction. It's only true progress when you're running toward something." He paused. "Right now, you don't know what you're running toward."

"Not yet, but I do know that life isn't a destination but a journey ... that one's going on my car for sure, now that I can afford a car."

"Ah, yes, the money. Enough for you to do whatever you want, assuming you know what you want to do."

"I'm pretty sure I'm going back to school in the fall."

"And I'm pretty sure your father will be happy about that," he said. "Don't you agree?"

"I guess that's probably true. I'm just not too sure how much it matters to me anymore whether he approves or disapproves of my choices."

It was funny because I used to think I didn't really care about his opinions, but I guess what I really was was mad at him, pretending not to care and then making decisions to try to get his attention, screwing up so that he'd have to notice. He'd said as much in his letter—that I'd made choices to make him proud or pissed off or sorry, but never for my own reasons. Now that I knew I could look after myself—I could get lost in a desert and survive, walk till my feet were bleeding and still get where I needed to go, even help someone else along the way—I felt as though I was really ready to make my own decisions, maybe hoping he'd approve, but not really needing him to.

I'd thought that would make me feel free, but in truth it made me feel a bit sad, too. Well, maybe I was never going to be close to my father—not in the way Andy and his dad were—but at least now I had some real friends. And not just L'Orange of Tunisia!

"Maybe the best I can hope for is that he doesn't think I'm a major disappointment," I told Larson.

"Think about what you did and how you did it," he said. "Think about the friendship and respect you've earned from Andy and Connor and Kajsa … and me. Just remember that the only person who can make you feel bad about yourself is you."

He reached over and took both my hands and held them in his. "Are you a disappointment?"

I took a moment to answer him. I wanted to be sure that I really believed what I was going to say.

"No, I'm not," I told him. "I did good. And I'm going to try to stay on course. On *my* course. All I have to do is figure out exactly where that course is going to take me."

"You don't have to think about the next seventy years. Take it one day at a time. What are you going to do tomorrow and the next day and the next and—?"

"I was sort of hoping to talk to you about that. When are you going back out into the desert?"

"In two weeks I have another group of young people who I'm taking on the same trek."

"Do you have space for one more person?" I asked. "I have the money to pay my way, so I can help with the next well. Can I come along?"

"Just tell me why … why do you want to do it when you've already done it?"

"The first time I did it because I had to, because I was forced to. This time it's for me. It's my decision, it's my walk."

"I'd be honoured to have you along."

"And I'd be honoured to be along. Besides, I have something I have to do. You'll think this is crazy."

"Try me."

I pulled L'Orange out of my pocket. He was all wrinkled and there was a bit of green growing on his peel.

"Are we going to pass through that oasis, the one where we met Mohammad?"

"That's on our planned route."

"I kind of promised L'Orange that I'd return him to where he belongs. That I'd plant him right there with the other orange trees."

"Why would I think that's crazy?" he asked. "I'll make another promise to you, and to L'Orange. Every time I go through that oasis, every time Mohammad or his clan go through that oasis, we'll water and tend to L'Orange. And in time, every time somebody picks an orange from that tree, it will be because of you."

I found myself choking up, tears coming to my eyes. I didn't want the guys to see me like that when they got back. And I didn't want them to feel sorry for me, nor did I want to take away the happiness they'd be feeling having just talked to their families ... and really, I guess I didn't want to hear about that when it was the very thing I didn't have.

"I'd better get to the hotel lobby and grab a taxi—I need to see the lawyer again to make the final arrangements," I said. "I know it isn't far from here, but for some reason, I just don't feel like walking right now."

He laughed. "I understand. So, we'll see you right after that?"

"Count on it."

I walked—at least hobbled—away.

The lobby was fairly crowded. It was a four-star hotel, and it was obviously popular with foreign businessmen. They all looked kind of the same to me—briefcase, suit and tie, shiny shoes. But when I looked again, I realized that one of the CEO types stood out from the others.

It was my father!

Larson had told me that he'd texted him to let him know we'd arrived safely. I figured he'd gotten that text in New York, but had he really come all the way to Tunis to meet me?

When he saw me, his face lit up and he crossed the lobby to join me. I didn't know quite what I was going to say to him, or what he might want to say to me, but I felt sure of one thing anyway—just as this was a chance for a new beginning for me, it was also the chance for a new start with him. Things could only get better from here. And we'd take it slowly, one step at a time.

AUTHOR'S NOTE

In the summer of 2009 a friend mentioned an acquaintance of his, Ray Zahab. Ray is one of the most incredible athletes this country has ever produced. He is an ultra-marathon runner who, along with his running mates, Kevin Lin and Charlie Engle, ran across the Sahara Desert from the Atlantic to the Pacific. This epic journey took 111 days in which they ran over 7500 kilometres, averaging more than sixty-two kilometres per day. This is almost beyond belief. Even more unbelievable, this is just one of his adventures. Ray has written what I hope is the first installment of his adventures in the fascinating book *Running for My Life* (Insomniac Press, 2007).

I arranged to meet Ray and went to a screening of their journey, *Running the Sahara*, produced and narrated by Matt Damon. After the screening Ray and I talked—not only about the Sahara run but also about something he was even more enthusiastic about: his newest initiative, Impossible2Possible (www.impossible2possible.com). This innovative program gives teens hands-on experience in leading expeditions around the world as Youth Ambassadors, communicating with participating schools by satellite technology and providing inspiration to reach beyond the limits and make positive change in the world. At that point he knew it would be a desert crossing and that it would take place the following spring.

I had no illusions that I could keep pace with these amazing athletes, but I knew I could participate and could walk along with them in their tracks. Over the next six months I went into training, walking no fewer than twenty kilometres per day, with my longest training walks almost fifty kilometres—in essence an "ultra-marathon." Through dozens of blisters, multiple pairs of shoes and numerous walking partners, I walked close to 4000 kilometres in preparation.

In April 2010 I joined Ray on a trip across the Sahara, traversing Tunisia. Guiding the expedition, along with Ray, was Marshall Ulrich. Marshall is one of the very few people on the entire planet who can be considered a "peer" of Ray's. As well as running across the United States, he has completed the Seven Summits (climbing the highest mountain on each continent), won numerous ultra-marathons through the harshest of environments, and was a champion in eco-challenge races around the world. These adventures are documented in his book, *Running on Empty* (Avery Publishing, 2011).

As this was an Impossible2Possible expedition, the leaders of this trip were four Youth Ambassadors: Andy, Connor, Jill and Kajsa. The characters in my book are, with their permission, named after them and elements of their personalities were embedded in my story, with the Kajsa character being an amalgamation of Jill and Kajsa. They are four high-performance athletes who are even better people than they are athletes. Connor has become an ongoing guest at our family functions as he attends the University of Guelph on a running scholarship, and Andy spent the first part of 2011 in our project in Kenya (www.creationofhope.com), teaching at a local school and living on the grounds of our orphanage.

The character Larson is a product of my imagination but he certainly shares many of the adventures of both Ray and Marshall, as well as their philosophic outlook on life. Ray has a boundless love of life and practically vibrates as he talks. Marshall is a calm observer of life—picture Buddha as an ultra-marathon runner.

Over an eight-day period they ran over 250 kilometres. I walked close to 200 of those kilometres. As I moved forward on blister-covered feet, the searing heat, the sandstorms, the scorpions, vipers and herds of wild camels became my reality.

Many of the things that happened on this trip are part of the story: sleeping in the tents, the